Hail

Mary

Book 1 of The Hail Raisers

By

Lani Lynn Vale

ISBN-13:
978-1983943225

ISBN-10:
1983943223

Dedication

To my youngest baby. I sure do hate when you're sick, but the love you give me when you are makes me cherish each and every cuddle.

Acknowledgements

Photographer: Furiousfogot

Model: Quinn Biddle

Editor: Ink It Out Editing, Ellie McLove, Danielle P.

CONTENTS

Kill Shot

Coup De Grace

The Uncertain Saints MC

Whiskey Neat

Jack & Coke

Kilgore Fire

Shock Advised

Flash Point

PROLOGUE

I miss you like an idiot misses the point.
-Dante's not-so-secret thoughts

Dante

Dante, honey. You need to just relax. Nothing will ever happen to us.

I woke with a start and bile creeping up the back of my throat.

I screamed.

The tiny cabin was empty except for my bed, so my anguished cries echoed off the empty walls.

This cabin… Lily and I had bought it as our retreat. Our home away from home. The place we would go when we needed time alone, away from the daily grind. Time to be together, just the two of us, with no interruptions, not even phone calls.

Dante, this place is perfect. Let's get it.

I made a noise akin to a wounded animal in the back of my throat and gritted my teeth.

I will not cry today. I will not cry today.

I'm a grown man! Grown men don't cry!

Everything, and I do mean everything, hurt.

I'd drunk myself into oblivion the night before, and I was feeling the after effects now.

I moaned as I rolled out of bed and walked stiffly to the bathroom.

My foot hit the corner of the door, and I cursed.

Dante, don't cuss in front of the girls. What are you going to do when they get in trouble at school for swearing when they fall down?

I ran to the toilet and threw up.

Today wasn't going to be a good day.

And, as if God, the life giver and the life taker, was listening, I felt a piece of hair tickling my chest.

I reached into my shirt and pinched what I thought was the hair, and pulled.

The hair...it was long. So long that I knew without a shadow of a doubt whose it would be.

The moment that it was exposed to the harsh, bright light of the bathroom, I bent over the toilet and threw up the last of the whiskey that I'd drank a few hours before.

I moaned and let my head rest against the lid of the toilet seat, turning it so that I could examine the strand of hair.

Even after all this time...after she'd been dead for so long...I still found her hair in my clothes.

Everywhere.

In my shirts, on my jackets. On my pillowcases.

God, she hadn't even stayed the night at this place, and her hair was on my sheets.

Sheets that I hadn't washed once since the last time she'd put them on the bed in anticipation of having a little alone time at our cabin.

I reached up blindly and flushed the toilet with the hand that wasn't clutching my dead wife's strand of hair, then sat back until I was on my butt.

Obviously, today wasn't going to be the day that I got my act together.

Hell, that day might never come.

I love you, Dante.

PROLOGUE II

A million men can tell a woman that she's beautiful, but the only time she will listen is when it comes from the man she loves.
-Fact of Life

Marianne

"Dante!"

"Don't talk, just feel me," he growled as he slid his shaft into me in long, full strokes.

I couldn't talk. I couldn't do anything but feel.

I don't know why he was telling me to just feel. Just feeling was all I could do whether I wanted to or not.

"I love you, Lily," Dante growled. "God, you've never felt so good."

I froze and then immediately started to shake as tears rolled down my face. "I-I'm not Lily. I'm Marianne, remember?"

The look of shock in his eyes as they met mine proved to me that he didn't.

Goddammit.

CHAPTER 1

*I can walk the walk, but please don't ask me to
jog the jog or run the run.*

-Meme sent to Dante from Baylor

Marianne

*The only time a goodbye is painful is when you know, for certain,
that it's the last one.*

I'd read those words in a magazine when I'd been nine months
pregnant with my baby.

I had no idea that, within weeks of having her, I'd be saying
goodbye. And I knew in my heart I'd never say hello again. It hurt.

I swallowed the lump in my throat.

It was, by far, the hardest thing I'd ever had to do.

I looked down at the little girl in the car seat, my reason for still
being alive.

Oh God, did it hurt.

It hurt so bad that I wasn't sure if I could draw my next breath.

A sound had me turning to the man that was standing on his
doorstep.

I'd only just found out where he lived. It'd taken me four precious
days to find him. Four days that I didn't have to give.

Why couldn't he be where he was supposed to be? Instead, he was living here, in this Godforsaken place.

Though, I did have to admit that when we'd been intimate, we'd done so at my old place. I hadn't exactly known that he wasn't living at the place across the street.

I got out of the car, walked around to the back door, and opened it.

He watched me the entire time, arms straining his shirt as he held them crossed over his chest.

His eyes felt like invasions of my privacy, and it physically hurt to have him this close to me and not touch that beautiful skin.

We'd spent one single, beautiful night together before he'd flipped out. One single, beautiful night that would forever be the best memory that I ever had.

CHAPTER 2

I don't need you, I have memes.

-Meme

Marianne

"Come on, baby," I whispered, pulling her out of the car seat and placing her on the bench seat next to it.

The next thing I did was unstrap the car seat itself from the car and set it on the grass.

He'd need all of it.

From what I'd been able to deduct over the last couple of days from my various sources, Dante lived minimally. He didn't have much of anything when it came to himself, why would he have anything when it came to a child?

So, I made sure to bring everything that I had.

I placed everything on the front lawn.

Diapers, bottles, a Pack 'n Play, her portable swing that I'd yet to get her to enjoy. It all went by the curb, making my tiny SUV that I'd stolen the night before look barren.

Once it was all out, I walked back to where my baby girl was sitting quietly in the seat and pulled her into my arms.

Through all of this, he only watched.

The moment my eyes met his, I felt his confusion.

It was almost palpable.

Why was I here? What was I doing?

I'd known that he'd been trying to find me.

Someone had tipped him off that I was pregnant. Someone had told him that we'd had a child together.

It was his brother who had found out, a man named Tobias, and it was his other brothers who continued to look into me.

However, them prodding into my life hadn't been what broke the camel's back. That had been something else. Another time, and another life.

God, how I'd hoped that it was all behind me forever. This was supposed to have been my second chance.

Yet here I was.

The moment I got to the bottom of the steps that Dante was standing on, I looked up at him.

He didn't move. Didn't speak. Didn't even look down at the baby I had in my arms.

"I have her medical information in a packet in her bag." I pulled in a deep, calming breath that didn't calm me in the least. "She needs you, Dante. I realize that you're broken, but she's not. Watch over her. You're my last hope. My only hope."

"Why now? What's going on?"

Dante's words felt like caresses on my overheated skin.

I sat my baby girl down on the swing next to where he was standing.

"Look up my name. You'll see."

With those cryptic words, I started to walk away.

"I don't know your name."

Those words hurt. In fact, it felt like that final, killing blow. The one that would leave me forever broken, never to be put back together again.

Nevertheless, I told him my name.

"Marianne Genevieve Garwood."

CHAPTER 3

I'm actually weirder than you think.

-Text from Baylor to Dante

Dante

I looked at the kid that was mine.

How did I know she was mine?

She looked exactly like my other children had.

All the way down to the bright blue eyes, the shock of white blonde hair, and the heart-shaped birthmark on her neck.

Looking down at this child was one of the hardest things I'd ever done in my life.

The moment that her eyes met mine, I realized the truth.

I, Dante Hail, was a coward.

Lily, my wife, was dead, and Jade and Toni, my two baby girls, had went with her.

Amy, my sister who was responsible for the accident that caused the death of my family, killed herself.

All of that was on me.

I would not be responsible for killing another living being.

I. Would. Not.

Pulling my computer out from where Lily had last left it—underneath the coffee table of all places—I opened it up and placed it on my lap.

Just the act of doing something I used to do when they were alive nearly sent me into a tailspin.

There was nothing to check on anymore. Not a goddamn thing.

Or, at least, there hadn't been last night.

Tonight would be different.

I looked over at the little girl, who was now sleeping, and pressed the power button.

It took a few seconds for the screen to blink on, and once it had booted up, what I saw caused my throat to tighten.

Now I remembered why I hadn't picked this computer up for two years.

A picture was on the screen.

One of my family.

I was in the middle while all three girls—my wife and children—kissed me.

It'd been our Christmas card the last Christmas we'd had together. The Christmas right before they'd died.

I was laughing my ass off as Jade, our youngest, gave me more than just kisses in the form of snot and slobber.

She was absolutely adorable.

A moan left my throat as I typed in the password: 1loveJadeToniLily.

Fuck.

As I waited for the laptop to boot up, all I could do was stare at that picture, remembering how happy I'd been.

By the time the main menu was up, I was on the verge of hyperventilating.

A whimper had my head turning, and I blinked as I saw the little girl staring at me with tears in her eyes.

"I… fuck."

Fuck.

I couldn't say fuck in front of a little girl!

Lily would've kicked my ass had I done that with her around!

I reached forward and picked the little girl up. Old muscle memory took over, and I cradled the little girl—my little girl—to my chest and looked down at her.

"Are you hungry?"

She blinked away her tears, and I studied her.

She really was adorable.

She had that fine, wispy baby hair that looked like it was spun from silk. Her curls were fuckin' everywhere, and she looked exactly like me and nothing like her mother.

Her mother had long brown hair, dark brown eyes, and an angular face.

This girl was all me.

The computer beeped, making me look away from the little girl, and to the screen.

I frowned, and my eyes took in the reminder on the computer: Change the air filter, lazy bones.

I grinned at my wife's reminder.

She wasn't even here anymore, and she was still taking care of me.

Goddammit.

I clicked the X on the corner of the reminder and went to the Chrome app, smiling when I heard Lily in my head say that she would never cheat on Internet Explorer.

Rolling my eyes at that funny memory—funny, but it still fucking hurt, even the happy memories—I typed in the woman's name into the Google search engine.

"Marianne Genevieve Garwood," I muttered as I typed.

The search instantly picked up hundreds of hits.

I clicked on the very first article—a news article from Jackson, Mississippi—and waited for it to load.

It didn't take long.

The headline read: Baby perishes in triple degree temperatures, locked in a car.

Drake Jackson Garwood, thirty-two, a prominent businessman for Corporate Crossroads, leaves infant son in car. The child, Raymond Jackson Garwood, succumbed to heat stroke due to the extreme temperatures in car.

I frowned.

Marianne Garwood, thirty, claims husband intentionally left their son in the car. We have not been able to reach her or Mr. Garwood for comment, but we did reach Mr. Garwood's attorney, who confirmed his client's assertions, cited a pending investigation and advised that all media inquiries would be handled by his office.

At press time, Drake Jackson Garwood has not been charged.

A chill passed over me as I back clicked and went to the next article. This one was dated six months later.

Drake Jackson Garwood acquitted for the involuntary manslaughter of his fourteen-week-old son. Mr. Garwood returns back to work but continues to work with other foundations to make sure that this doesn't happen to any other father.

Something about that soured my stomach and made it summersault.

I back clicked and went to the next hit.

Marianne Garwood missing.

Marianne Garwood kidnapped.

Marianne Garwood's car found in lake, husband inconsolable.

The more I read, the angrier I became.

I knew I didn't have the whole story.

Knew it. Felt it in my bones.

My fucking heart hurt for Mary.

I closed my eyes and dropped my head to the back of the couch.

The baby in my arms cried.

CHAPTER 4

*The closest I get to a spa day is when the steam
from the dishwasher hits me in the face.*

-Cobie's secret thoughts

Cobie

Six months later

"I want you to help me die."

I looked over at my friend.

"What?"

"I want you to help me die," she repeated.

I was stunned.

"Marianne…"

"Please," she whispered. "It hurts."

"But your husband…"

"Wants me to suffer."

That sounded like her pain talking.

"Honey," I said softly. "You have to fight this."

"I'm dead already. It's only a matter of time." She took in a deep breath. "It hurts."

I didn't know what to say.

"You haven't even seen this week's scans!" I whispered.

She looked away.

"Cobie." She closed her eyes for long moments. "I got them back yesterday."

"But you just told your husband that you—"

She interrupted me. "I lied. I got them back yesterday. The cancer... it's spread."

"But this experimental treatment..."

She laughed harshly. "It's not experimental. It's bullshit. Drake found this quack doctor to talk out of his ass. I keep going to my real doctor because I know that whatever bullshit this quack is shooting me up with isn't working. I... Cobie... I think it's just a show. They're acting like they're helping me when in reality they're not doing anything. He hasn't even looked at my scans, not even once. He just keeps saying he's going to make me all better."

I didn't know what to say.

Hearing her say this about Drake of all people was alarming.

Drake was everything any woman would want in a husband... wasn't he?

I didn't know what to say.

"Okay, honey," I said. "I believe you... but what you're asking of me... I can't do that."

She looked down at her hands.

"It hurts," she whispered. "And the cancer has metastasized. It's now in my lungs, heart tissue, my liver, and it's spreading into my reproductive system."

Hearing this news was devastating.

I thought that she was going to be the one to beat it all.

It wasn't supposed to be me. Never, not in a million years, would I have thought that I would come back from stage four cancer. But I had. I'd done it, and I thought that she could, too.

But still, what she was asking me to do… that just wasn't me. I couldn't kill my best friend, no matter what the circumstances were.

Especially not with all the secrets she'd been keeping from me lately. Hell, I barely even knew who she was at this point. It was downright scary.

"I can't." A tear slipped free. "Please, don't ask that of me. Please."

Marianne looked away, her bald head shining brightly in the harsh glow of the hospital lights.

"Marianne…"

Marianne looked back at me. "It was a selfish thing to ask."

It wasn't.

I knew the kind of pain she was in. I had been there at one point myself.

If what she was feeling was anything like what I felt… I could even totally sympathize.

Before I could say anything else to her, the alarm on my phone rang, reminding me that I had my own doctor's appointment today.

Check-up day.

"I love you, Mare."

Marianne held her hands out to me, and I went to them willingly.

Pressing my forehead against hers, I tried to instill some of my strength into her through our hug.

"I love you, too, Cobie."

Giggling through my tears, I walked out of her room.

When she'd called me today from the hospital, I had a minor freak out.

She'd told me that the doctor had admitted her for dangerous dehydration levels, and I came as soon as I'd heard.

I just wished I didn't have my own appointment today. I didn't want to leave her there, especially not with those thoughts that I knew were swirling around her head.

I want you to help me die.

I shivered from head to toe.

I never thought I'd hear her say that. Not Marianne, my best friend. The only person I could really rely on in this world.

I swiped at my tears and cleared my throat.

I passed a man in the hall. He was carrying a little girl in his arms.

Our eyes met, and instantly I saw him take in my tears.

He stopped.

"You okay?"

I smiled tremulously. "I'll be okay."

Then I walked away, hoping that guy wasn't going into that cancer unit to see someone of his own.

He looked like a man that had seen enough pain.

How I knew that, I didn't know. But I did.

I had no idea that the man that I'd spoken with that day would help like he did.

No idea.

But I'd find out.

And it wasn't going to be good.

CHAPTER 5

*I'm proud to say that my house doesn't have any
unhealthy snacks... because I ate them all.*

-Cobie's secret thoughts

Cobie

6 months later

Marianne was dead.

I looked over at the coffin, wondering if I'd ever get over her loss.

She was my best friend and confidant.

Why did I get to live and Marianne didn't?

What made me so special?

She had a husband—sure, she'd told me he wasn't the greatest man in the world, but that wasn't abnormal—and a child.

Though the child she'd told me about wasn't with her husband. It was with some man that she met while she and her husband were separated.

"Hello, Cobie."

I shivered at the words coming out of that mouth.

It wasn't a good shiver, either.

I turned to see Drake standing there, looking at me with concern.

Drake was incredibly good-looking. Tall, about six feet, and in good shape. His hair was salt and pepper, graying more to silver along his temples. I always felt that he and Marianne seemed to be that golden couple. The one that you couldn't help but look at when you walked into the room because they were just that beautiful.

"Hi, Drake." I tried to smile.

"Are you okay?"

I shrugged. "I guess maybe that should be me asking that of you."

His grin was small.

"I'm fine." He smiled then. "Would you like to come over?"

I frowned. "I'm sorry, Drake. Were you having a memorial after the services? I didn't know. I have to babysit tonight."

That was a lie. I didn't have to babysit anyone. I just didn't want to do anything with him.

Drake winked. "No, no memorial. Marianne didn't want one. She never wanted me to dwell on her death. I felt that a memorial was dwelling."

Dwelling. Was remembering a person for what she used to be dwelling? I didn't think so.

"Okay," I smiled. "I'll be seeing you around, Drake."

And I did. Much more than I would have wanted to.

But, I couldn't help but feel bad for my dead best friend's husband.

It was all innocent, right?

Still contemplating that, I walked away without looking back.

My eyes looked up at just the right moment, and I frowned when I saw someone that looked vaguely familiar.

He was tall with close-cropped, dirty blond hair, and he was well-built but incredibly scary looking. For some reason, I could picture his eyes as being bright blue.

How would I know the color of his eyes?

As I got closer, I saw him get on a bike and start it up.

Once I got to my car, I halted beside it with my hand on the door handle and stared.

Why was he so familiar?

But before my mind could make the connection, he rode off, leaving me watching him go.

My belly already in knots, I got into my car and started her up.

But instead of thinking about Drake or Marianne, I thought about that man.

Why did it feel like he'd just stolen something from me?

CHAPTER 6

I don't understand why gyms have mirrors. I
know I need some work, that's why I'm here.

-Cobie's secret thoughts

Cobie

Six months later

"Let me help," Drake Garwood, my best friend's widower,
pleaded.

I shook my head.

"You can't make me do this, Drake," I apologized. "I don't *want*
treatment."

Drake had been there for me, just like I'd been there for him, for
six months now since Marianne's death.

Those six months hadn't always been great.

In fact, after a certain time period—about four months after his
wife's death—Drake had started to court me. Or at least he tried to,
anyway.

I didn't want anything to do with that—or him.

I still wasn't over Marianne's death, and it bothered me that Drake
would think that I would want anything to do with him like that.

It felt like a slap in the face to Marianne.

So, I'd done my level best to keep him at arm's length, but he did everything he could to push against the boundaries I'd set.

And now, with the news that I'd gotten just yesterday, he was already pushing to help me.

I didn't want his help.

In fact, I wanted nothing to do with his help because having his help meant that I'd have to face cancer again, and I didn't want to face it.

I just wanted to breathe easy.

Something I hadn't been able to do since I was informed that I had cancer when I'd gone to the ER for shortness of breath.

Ever since, I hadn't known what breathing easy was.

I just wanted to breathe.

I couldn't breathe.

"I'll see you later, Drake," I apologized as I backed away. "Thank you for the ride home from the hospital."

Drake watched me go up the front steps of my walk, and the moment I reached the door, I hurriedly pushed it open and locked it behind me.

If there had been anybody else in the world that I could have contacted right then, I would have.

However, I had nobody.

My co-workers, although nice, didn't really know much about me.

I'd been a nurse for six years, and four of those years I'd been in the same labor and delivery unit, yet I was no closer to my co-workers then I had been when I started.

Though, I had a feeling that a lot of that had to do with me.

Women just never seemed to like me.

Never.

That's why, when I met Marianne after she'd given birth to her son, I'd been happy for her extension of friendship.

We'd hit it off well, and during the time that she battled postpartum depression followed shortly after by her battle with cancer—which coincided with mine—I was happy to call her friend.

Now, I had nobody.

Not a single person.

No one.

I looked around at my house, wondering who I would donate it all to once I was gone.

Maybe the historical district.

They'd been hounding me about this house, and all of my grandfather's things, for a very long time now.

They wanted me to restore the house, while I, on the other hand, wanted to remember the house how it was when my grandfather had lived in it.

I missed my grandfather.

He'd been the one who raised me, and not a day went by that I did not miss seeing him.

He'd died six years ago, now.

My eyes lit on the picture of him and my grandmother on their wedding day sixty-five years ago that was hanging above the fireplace.

He looked so happy.

So, so happy.

I couldn't see much of my grandmother's face due to my grandfather's massive hand covering most of it as he held her mouth to his, but I could imagine that she was practically beaming just like he was.

I wiped the single tear that fell from my eye and went to step away from my door when a knock sounded at the back of my house.

Frowning, I moved through the hallway, around through the dining room, and stopped in the kitchen.

There was a man standing at my back door.

A blond man.

A familiar looking blond man.

I scowled.

Where did I know him from?

Before I could so much as ask him why he was at my back door and where I knew him from, he reared forward. His arms went around my waist, and suddenly I was no longer alone in my house.

I opened my mouth to scream, but he was there, his hand over my face, shushing me. "Stop."

I froze.

Terror was filling my veins, but a shiver of something else rushed through me, too.

This man, he was hot.

Let's just get that out in the open.

However, hot or not, he was in my house, uninvited. I didn't know him, and I wasn't fucking stupid.

There wasn't going to be any misconstrued feelings from me. No, sir. I was well and truly freakin' the fuck out.

"Don't scream."

I nodded because who the hell wouldn't agree when a big man, one who was over six-foot tall—and I say that number because my grandfather had been that size and I didn't have to strain my neck to look up at him like I had to do with this man—and he was staring me straight in the eye. He didn't have to say what he would do if I did scream, which I wouldn't.

"I'm not going to hurt you," he rasped, letting go of my face, as well as me entirely.

I blinked, unsure what to do.

Did I ask him what he was doing there? Did I tell him that I wanted him to leave? Though, that one would be stupid to ask, because I damn well knew he wouldn't leave. He wouldn't be there if he didn't have some sort of agenda.

"Call Drake and tell him you won't be meeting him for lunch like you'd planned. You're not feeling well."

I blinked, opened my mouth to reply and tell him that there wouldn't be lunch with him ever, but he shook his head. "Trust me."

I laughed harshly at that. "I have much more reason to trust Drake than I do you. You've forced yourself into my home. There is no trusting you, moron."

The man's eye twitched.

"You got a computer?"

I blinked, then nodded, "If I show you where it's at, you'll take it and leave?"

41

He rolled his eyes as if I'd just asked him the stupidest question on earth.

"No, I'm gonna show you what your boyfriend Drake does."

Brows furrowing, I watched as he walked to it, flipped it open, and glared at the background photo.

Yeah, I wasn't really all that great looking in that one. It was the day that Marianne had come home. Marianne, who'd been kidnapped straight out of her home.

Her long hair was wispy, flying around her face like a freakin' hair commercial. Her crystal blue eyes were wide and smiling, and her lips were plump and pink.

She was beautiful…and then there was me.

Me? Well, I wasn't much to look at. I was average, not tall but not short, either. Around five-foot-five or so. I had long brown hair—well, at one point in time I did. Now it fell to just barely below my chin now that it'd started growing back after my chemo and radiation treatments. I had muddy brown eyes the color of dirt, freckles all over my face that weren't the kind that were considered 'cute' but were instead what I'd call 'too much.' I used to have a healthy-looking, somewhat muscular figure. Not fat, but not skinny, either. Then I got cancer, went through chemo, hadn't able to keep a damn thing down for months and lost way too much weight.

I'd just started putting that weight back on when I got sick again and started having shortness of breath—which had prompted my visit to the emergency room. The ER had run some tests, and I now had a mammogram scheduled in two days thanks to my left breast being swollen and red.

I'd thought it was just the flu.

I should've known it wasn't.

My life wasn't all that great.

It'd been hard from the day I was born up until now.

My mom left me with my grandparents the day I was born. I never knew who my father was. When I was seven, I was run over by a car. When I was twelve, I tried to run away, but instead of actually running away, I instead managed to get myself stuck in a storm drain, nearly drowning when a torrential downpour began. At the age of sixteen, I got pregnant and almost died from an ectopic pregnancy, and in the process, I, of course, lost the baby. At nineteen, I lost my grandmother. At twenty-four, two days before my nursing graduation, my grandfather died.

Then, at twenty-eight, I'd found out that I had stage four ovarian cancer.

Just when I thought I had it beaten, I find out that I now had breast cancer. Oh, and let's not forget about the psycho standing in my room, doing something with my computer.

I scratched my chin and started to back up toward the back door, but stopped when he suddenly turned the computer to me.

"What is that?" I gasped, rushing forward.

"*That* is Drake."

I knew that. I could see that. Drake was standing outside the house that I'd let him use.

"What is he doing?" I whispered.

He pointed to the truck and ignored my question. "Look at this one."

Then he switched to the next picture.

Drake was hauling open the door, and inside the truck, there were floor-to-ceiling crates. The only thing I'd ever seen in crates were guns, so I was hoping that my mind was just filling in the blanks, rather than knowing for a certainty.

Surely there could be something else inside those boxes.

"What?"

"I think he's allowing his house to be used as a base of some sort."

"Base?"

"Or a storage facility." He paused. "I don't fuckin' know. I do know that whatever he's doing, he's doing it at night so no one can see him. I also know that when he sees these people that make these deliveries at a restaurant in town, they don't acknowledge that they know each other. Seems legitimately shady to me."

I agreed.

"I know that one," I pointed to the man with the Asian features. "He's a trainer at the gym where I used to work out."

My captor grunted.

"None of this makes sense," I muttered to myself. "None of it."

"What sense do you need to make of this to know he's doing something bad?" he practically spat. "The man is a fuckin' douche."

"Whatever he has going on here can be verified rather quickly." I walked away from him and to the set of keys on the counter but paused in turning for a few seconds when a wave of dizziness washed over me.

"Cobie?"

I shook it off and raised the keys in the air.

"I own that house."

"I know."

"You do?"

He nodded. "That was at least easy to find. But, even if tax records for property weren't public knowledge, Marianne told me before she passed."

"Marianne…"

And then it all clicked, where I'd seen him.

I'd seen him for the first time in the hospital as I'd left Marianne's room. The second time I'd seen him had been at her funeral.

"You."

He winced.

"Took me three freakin' months to find you," he said. "And then three months of looking into you and Drake to decide that maybe you weren't in on it."

"Why do you care if I'm in on it or not?"

He looked down at his hands. "Marianne asked me to take care of you."

"What?"

"She told me to take care of you," he repeated.

"Why?" I blurted.

Not that he'd have to deal with that promise for much longer.

Stage two breast cancer meant that I would possibly die by the end of next year, according to my doctor, if I didn't try to treat it.

And honestly, I was just so damn tired.

I was tired of fighting.

Tired of losing.

I wanted some peace.

Even if that peace came in the form of death.

At least in death, I knew that I wouldn't suffer anymore. I knew that I wouldn't wake up and realize that I was alive to live another day in pain.

Since I'd battled cancer before, I knew what would happen.

I knew that my life would suck for however long the doctor deemed necessary for me to do the chemo and radiation treatments.

Plus, I would still need to have a double mastectomy if the chemo and radiation did its job and killed all the cancerous cells in my body. And I say that 'if' cautiously since there was still a chance that it wouldn't work, and I would go through all these treatments—all the fighting—only to succumb to the cancer. I just didn't know if I had it in me or if I even wanted to do it anymore.

There was nobody left to make me want to fight—to convince me that the pain was worth it.

Not even knowing that there was something going on with Drake, and this man was trying to let me in on said information, was going to make me change my mind.

Suddenly, I was just freakin' tired.

"What's your name?" I blurted, suddenly needing to know who this man was.

"Dante Hail."

Dante Hail.

"What put all those shadows in your eyes, Dante Hail?"

His entire being stilled.

His eyes on me. The breath in his chest. The absent tapping of his fingers against the countertop next to the computer.

Everything.

"Some time I'll tell you of my own personal hell," he said. "But now's not that time."

"I could be dead by next year," I told him bluntly. "Let's make sure you tell me before that time comes."

He blinked.

"What do you mean, dead?"

I fought through the exhaustion. Through the wave of knowledge that stuck with me as I moved toward Dante, and shrugged.

"I have breast cancer," I admitted. "It's fairly advanced, and without treatment, the doctor doesn't think I'll make it through the year."

He stared at me for a long time, his gaze so damn intense that it almost made me squirm.

"Dying is the coward's way out."

I laughed at that. "Maybe."

He opened his mouth to argue. "Why wouldn't you do the treatment?"

I dropped the keys next to his hand and stared up into his eyes.

"Why would I?" I asked, pausing to study his eyes as I said what I had to say next. "Whatever put those shadows in your eyes lets me know that you probably have a good idea what it feels like to have nothing left."

His hand came up to my cheek, and only his index finger ran along the line of my cheekbone. "Used to think I had nothing," he answered. "Found out about a year and a half ago that I did."

I smiled sadly. "I'm glad that you do."

He pushed the keys away from his hand and took a step back.

"Come on," he urged, reaching forward and almost brushing my face with his shirt.

Then he yanked the jump drive out of the computer.

I blinked.

"You just took the jump drive out of the computer without ejecting it first," I told him. "That's a good way to corrupt the data you have there."

He shrugged. "Sometimes I like to live dangerously."

I rolled my eyes.

"I guess if that's what you think dangerous is, then maybe we shouldn't be going any further into this investigation without someone who knows what they're doing."

His lips twitched.

"Honey, I was in the Air Force. You're not going to find anyone who knows what they're doing more than I do."

I laughed. "If you say so."

He took a hold of my arm and pulled me along in his wake.

"Where are we going now?"

He let go of my arm long enough to twist the lock on the back side of my door, and then pushed me out into the warm autumn air.

"We're going to get a few answers."

Then he was pulling me along with him.

"Where is that?"

He grunted something, and I had to tug on his hand to get him to repeat himself. "What?"

"Kilgore."

CHAPTER 7

*I don't always pass slow drivers, but when I do I
check to see if they look as stupid as they drive.*

-Dante's secret thoughts

Dante

If what she said was true, then this woman wasn't anything to be
worried about, but I was skeptical.

I'd witnessed that scene out front.

Drake had his hands on her, and she hadn't protested the move.

I wanted to trust her. Really, I did.

But I didn't trust anyone. Not anymore.

Not after I trusted the one person that I always thought I could
trust, and she ripped my life to shreds by uttering one tiny little lie.

And learning that she had cancer? I wasn't so sure what to think.

Who wouldn't try to fight if there was a chance? This woman was
young. Just barely thirty. I'd looked at her driver's license while
she'd been in the gas station using the restroom at the last rest stop.

She still had a long life full of events to look forward to—like
marriage and kids. *Those would be the best years of her life, and
she was just going to give it up?*

That seemed off to me.

However, without actually seeing her doctor, I could only go by what she was telling me, and that wasn't much.

However, Rafe, my contact with whatever secret organization he belonged to, was less than ten minutes away and would hopefully be able to fix that. Soon.

This woman, Cobie Cavanagh, was an enigma.

There was something about her that was making me insanely curious, and I didn't fuckin' like that.

I liked being distant from other people. I liked knowing that I wasn't affected by getting too close to them.

So what if she didn't want to do her cancer treatments. So what if she had cancer.

I shouldn't fuckin' care.

But I did.

It was driving me goddamn insane, thinking that she was going to purposefully not treat this disease that would eventually kill her.

The idea of her not being here on this earth next year was fucking hurting.

It shouldn't hurt.

In fact, if I was living my life right, nothing should hurt anymore.

Mary was fucking ruining me.

And that was that.

She was making me care when the last thing on this planet I wanted to do was have feelings for another human being. Some person who could up and die on me, leaving me with yet another open and bleeding wound that I had no hope of repairing.

"Do you know where we're going?"

I nodded, not bothering to look over at this Cobie chick with her soulful brown eyes and the cutest goddamn freckles I'd ever seen.

Her hair was brown and barely brushing her chin.

I wanted to touch it, which was the last thing on this earth that I needed to do.

What I needed to do was collect myself, build my wall higher, and continue not to feel.

What I was going to do was touch her goddamn hair.

I couldn't help myself.

I reached up and grabbed one of the strands.

It felt like silk between my fingers.

"You had a bug in your hair," I lied, pulling my hand back like it'd been burned.

Her eyes went wide, and she immediately started to sift her fingers through her hair where I'd just touched.

"Oh my God!" she gasped. "Really? Did you get it?"

"Ladybug," I continued to lie.

I tried to think of something that wouldn't gross her out, but she seemed to pale even further, causing my brows to rise.

"Gross," she whispered, then did a full, head to toe, entire body shiver.

"Ladybugs aren't gross," I told her, taking the next turn a little too fast, causing her to lean slightly into the passenger side door.

"Yes, they are," she disagreed with me. "They're really, super-duper gross."

"Why do you say that?"

Now she had me curious.

I hated being curious.

It made me ask questions, which inevitably made me get closer to the person despite my not wanting to get closer. But sometimes my curiosity won out, and this was one of those times.

"There was this one time when my grandfather, grandmother, and I were camping."

I nodded, urging her to continue without saying it verbally.

"Anyway, we were in the RV, and I was going to the bathroom."

My brows rose.

"I was… you know… and I decided to do a courtesy flush."

I blinked, and she blushed.

"Never mind."

"You have to finish it now."

I didn't know where she was going with this, but she had my interest piqued.

She shrugged, then continued as if what she was saying wasn't the least bit embarrassing. Only her blush betrayed her and made her freckles stand out even more starkly on her face.

"I flushed, and I don't know if you've ever been in an RV before, but it's gravity fed. You push a lever on the base of the toilet, and the hole opens, letting the stuff fall through."

I nodded in understanding. I knew exactly what she was talking about.

Lily and I had an RV… I viciously shut those thoughts down.

I couldn't think about my wife right now.

Not when I was trying to appear normal and sane.

"Anyway, so I flushed, and I don't know if the ladybugs had somehow gotten into the tank or what, but the moment that I opened the hole, a swarm of them came out from the tank below and went everywhere. And when I say everywhere, I mean all over my lady bits. When I stood up, they just kept coming. They swarmed the room, I had to slap them off my junk. It was god awful."

I couldn't help it.

I laughed.

It sounded rusty like the sound was being pulled out of a rarely used squeaking door, but it was a laugh, nonetheless.

It actually felt kind of good.

I could just see her, screeching and hollering, as she tried to get ladybugs off of her pussy.

"I'm still traumatized," she said. "One even bit me on one of my petals."

"Your petals." I grinned.

She nodded. "My petals."

I rolled my eyes.

"That sucks, honestly," I said. "But I guess it could've been worse."

"How?" she challenged.

My brows dipped low. "It could've been a wasp nest in there. Just imagine being stung on your 'petals' by one of those."

Her eyes went wide. "Dear God. That's sick! You're sick. I could've died! Now I'll never be able to go to the bathroom in an RV again!"

I just shook my head and went back to driving, not saying another word for the rest of the drive to our destination.

"You think I'm crazy," she said as we pulled up to the gates of Free long minutes later. "I know you do. But it's a fear, and most fears don't tend to be rational."

Some fears were rational.

But before I could argue with her, the gate swung open, and a man walked out of the office that the driveway led up to.

He had a wrench in his hand, and his eyes were narrowed on us, calculating everything in a single sweep.

Former military.

Had to be.

I pulled to a stop in the middle of the lot, seeing with my own eyes that the guy was wondering why I was there.

I was driving a company tow truck, and it was quite obvious that I had no reason for being where I was.

"Can I help you?"

Maybe calling would've been the better way to go.

Yet, it'd been a split-second decision, and I'd gotten the info from my brother on the way there.

Baylor had his own problems when it came to his wife, and they had led to his own trip to this same place to ask his own questions.

Baylor had told me he'd asked them about Marianne, yet they wouldn't give him anything, citing that whatever problems his wife, Lark, had, they looked like middle-school problems compared to Marianne's. And I believed them. Now.

But I needed more information.

Marianne hadn't only gotten a promise about Cobie out of me. She'd also charged me with protecting Mary, and at this point in my life, I'd charge through the gates of hell to make sure she was safe.

She was all I had left, and I was going to make sure that she had everything she needed, that she was safe and happy and healthy.

Anything she needed, she was going to get.

I'd make sure of it.

"My name is Dante." I got out of the truck and held out my hand.

The man took it, shook it, and dropped it without giving his name.

I felt a grin tug at the corner of my lips.

"I'm here to see someone," I said. "Sam Mackenzie."

The man's eyes narrowed.

"What do you want to see him for?"

I admired his hesitancy.

"The mother of my daughter, Marianne Garwood, died six months ago. She told me that her daughter would always be in danger from her ex-husband and that if I ever felt that things were getting out of hand, to find y'all."

Cobie inhaled behind me.

I'd left that part out. *Oops.*

The man's eyes narrowed on the woman who was standing practically all the way behind me, and then flicked back to me.

"I'm Sam," he said, his shoulders slumping slightly. "Get in the car and drive around to the big gray building. Follow the drive until you get to it. I'll be there in a minute."

I nodded, then gestured for Cobie, who'd followed my lead, to get into the car.

"You didn't tell me you had her daughter."

"My daughter, too," I muttered. "And you didn't ask."

She didn't have anything to say to that, and I didn't bother to explain myself. She'd learn everything along with the rest of them in just a few minutes anyway.

***

Twenty minutes later we were in a conference room. Cobie was sitting next to me, and we were waiting for the men to arrive.

Rafe, a man who—among other things—worked with my brother, was sitting across the table from us, watching with unconcealed interest.

I ignored him. When I'd left Hostel earlier in the day, he'd been working.

Now he was here.

He needed to be fired.

"Why is Drake living in your house?"

She grimaced.

"Apparently, Drake had to sell his house to help pay for Marianne's cancer treatments. I felt bad, so I let them use the house that I was living in before my grandfather left me this place."

"He pay rent?"

She nodded. "He insisted, actually. A thousand a month."

I grunted.

"Thousand a month is pretty steep. What part of town?"

That came from Rafe.

"Wildwood."

He blinked. "You moved out of Wildwood, to a house in the historical district, and you're letting someone live in it for a thousand a month?"

It was obvious that he didn't agree with her decision.

"She was my best friend, and he was her husband. What did you want me to do, let them live on the streets while she battled cancer?"

Rafe shrugged.

The door to the office slammed, and soon three men were making their way into the conference room, taking various chairs around the table and sitting.

All of them were big.

They were all Army.

I could tell by the tattoos that each one of them had on their arm.

Huh, go figure.

"This is Jack," Sam, who'd taken a seat directly across from me, pointed to his left.

I nodded my head at Jack, taking in his dark eyes and even darker hair. "Nice to meet you."

Jack didn't reply.

"This is Max," Sam gestured to his right. "They both worked on Marianne's case."

I didn't bother offering a hello to Max. He was scowling at me like I'd done something wrong.

"And I think you know Rafe."

I nodded. "I do."

"Tell us what's going on."

I looked over at Cobie before turning back to Sam.

"It's easier to start from the beginning," I muttered.

"Please do," Rafe said sarcastically.

I narrowed my eyes at him.

"Why am I giving you a paycheck when you're not even doing your job?"

Rafe's lips tipped up. "I am doing my job. Right now, in fact."

My brows rose, and I pulled out my phone, looking at the log of calls and pick-ups we were supposed to be filling right now. "You are? Because right now, I show that there are four outstanding recoveries that need to be made. You're on the clock, am I correct?"

I might not have put in the hours that I should have over the last couple of years, but that didn't mean that I didn't keep tabs on my business. Not to mention that before Lily had passed, we'd created an app that literally showed us all impending pick-ups when they were entered into the computer—and still did, to that fact.

Rafe grinned. "Sure."

I growled under my breath and turned to Sam, who showed no surprise at either Rafe being there when he shouldn't be, or me knowing that Rafe shouldn't be there.

"I had a one-night stand with Marianne when she lived across the street from my brother. After leaving that night, she disappeared, then showed back up with a baby she said was mine. She told me that she couldn't take care of her any longer and that it was my turn."

Neither Sam nor anyone else at the table for that matter, said anything in response to that.

The woman at my side made a choking sound in the back of her throat, but I didn't look at her.

"She told me to look her up on the internet," I continued. "Then, a while later I tracked her down. She got two promises out of me, and then I left. I didn't see her again unless you count her funeral."

Sam cursed.

"What were those promises?"

"They were to watch over this one," I indicated to Cobie with a tilt of my head. "And to watch over our girl. If I ever suspected that there was something brewing, I was to come to you."

"What do you think is going on?"

That came from Jack.

I leaned over and pulled out an envelope that was folded multiple times. Once I unfolded it, I pulled the letter I'd received out and laid it out flat on the table before turning it around for the men across from me to see.

"That's a letter from an attorney," I said. "When Marianne died, she left everything she had to Mary. In doing so, she also put Mary on Drake's radar."

"What did Marianne leave Mary?"

I pulled out my copy of the will, laid it out flat, and pushed it forward for them to see.

"Eight million dollars. Two estates, one in Massachusetts and one in England. Multiple automobiles."

"If he had that much money, why did they have to rent a house from me?"

59

I looked over at Cobie then and shrugged. "*He* didn't have any money. Nothing. Mary is the beneficiary. I am the co-beneficiary until Mary is of age. Drake had nothing because Marianne made sure of that. If I had my guess, you resembled a cash cow like Marianne did, and Drake was trying to use you until he could figure out how to get his wife's money."

"She had to know that by naming Mary in her will, she would be shining a spotlight on her," Max added his two cents.

I nodded and blew out a frustrated breath.

"Yeah, pretty much," I agreed. "I'm in over my head at this point. I was in the Air Force. I've seen my share of clusterfucks, but I have a really bad fucking feeling right now. I've been sitting here, twiddling my thumbs, for almost six months, trying to make sense of some of this stuff, but I'm not getting anywhere. I need help. I need to know if Drake is as bad as he appears to be because I have a feeling that once this one lets Drake know she isn't going to be his cash cow, he'll come after Mary next. Plus, Drake knows where and how to find me very easily."

CHAPTER 8

*Make your weird light shine bright… so other
weirdos can find you.*

-Bumper Sticker

Cobie

My mind was working at about a thousand miles an hour.

However, I was stuck on one thing in particular.

I am not anyone's cash cow!

Sam sat back in his chair. "How do you know Drake?"

Dante's mouth worked, causing his jaw muscles to flex.

"He used to be my brother's best friend," he grunted. "At first, I wasn't too sure about it. But his name, Drake Garwood, isn't so fucking common. I knew it was too big of a coincidence. Then, when I had to go to the reading of the will in Mary's stead, I recognized Drake immediately."

"Does your brother know?"

He shook his head.

"No."

"Are you going to tell him?" I asked.

I was really curious. Why wouldn't his brother know this? It was his niece who was affected, after all.

He shook his head again. "Not yet. I don't have enough proof. I don't want to jump the gun yet, then ruin whatever friendship they have left if it's not what I think it is. Reed still talks to him on occasion. He's made it a point to keep up with him through the years, and I don't want to ruin that relationship without knowing the full story. Maybe he's just caught up in this. Maybe he's just in over his head and needs a way out. Maybe he won't do anything at all, but I just can't take a chance with Mary like that."

I licked my lips and blew out a breath.

"Marianne told me once that Drake scared her," I hesitated. "Then another time, after their son was killed, she lost it, blaming it on Drake. She said that he did it on purpose, and even went as far as to tell the cops, as well as every single news outlet that covered the baby's death, what she thought."

He stared at me unnervingly.

"She also told me, about a week before she died, that Drake had her going to some doctor that she thought was 'pretending' to cure her cancer." I licked my lips again. God, why were they so dry? "He's an MD, I looked him up after her death. I couldn't get her words out of my brain. But the thing is…"

"But," Dante drawled.

"But that's all that I could find on him. There's no case studies or articles or anything on these experimental miracle treatments he supposedly developed. There's literally nothing out there on him at all."

The man scowled.

"I'm not going to say that I'm good at finding shit on people, because I'm not. What I've found out is by asking people stuff, like I did with you. I don't have any computer skills what-so-fucking-ever. That's why I wanted to come talk to these guys. I need to know what the fuck is going on."

"Because of what you showed me earlier?"

"Yes."

I didn't know what to say to that.

"Why now?"

His jaw clenched at my question.

"Honestly?"

I blinked.

"Yes," I paused. "Why would I ask you a question and not want you to be honest?"

He chuckled.

It was the second time he'd done anything like that in the entire hour that I'd been in the same space as him.

"Tell me about the pictures."

"What pictures?" the beautiful man that Sam had introduced as Rafe asked.

Dante reached into his pocket, pulled out the jump drive and then slid it across the table.

Rafe immediately reached for it and slid it farther down the table to the man called Jack.

Jack took it, stood up, and walked over to a panel on the wall where he plugged the jump drive in.

"Hope that the data isn't corrupted," I muttered mostly to myself.

Dante gave me a look, and I found myself blinking my eyes innocently at him.

He rolled his and turned when a screen descended at the front of the room.

"This is like the future," I uttered to myself once again.

Jack turned and offered me a smile.

"Not the future," he said. "Just technology that is advancing every single day."

I didn't argue with that, mostly because it was so true.

Every two years, a new iPhone came out, and every two years, I got a new one. The newer models weren't really all that different from the older ones. At least that's how it seemed until you compared an older iPhone to your newest one, side-by-side.

Something I'd actually done myself a few weeks ago while I'd been digging through my grandpa's old desk and found one of my old phones.

The fucker had even turned on and run after I'd charged it. I was purely amazed and sat there for twenty minutes looking at the old pictures. Of course, the pictures were tiny compared to the phone I carried now. Pictures that I'd somehow lost, and smiled for hours as I thought about the things I used to do as a teenager. Camping with my grandparents. Fishing with Grandpa. Cooking with Grandma.

God, there'd been so many freakin' pictures of pies that I'd had to laugh.

"Tell me where you were when you took these pictures."

Sam's comment brought me back to the present, and I stared at the same picture that Dante had shown me earlier.

"Right outside her house."

"You live there with him?"

Dante shook his head. "This is her old place. She rented it to him."

I nodded my head, and we explained what had happened again to them.

"At first, I started watching her place, thinking she was living there. When I realized Drake was there, I'd intended to leave it alone, not wanting to draw attention to myself. But then I started noticing strange things, and I couldn't help myself."

"See that number, Sam?"

Max's question had me straining my eyes to see where Max was pointing.

"No. Where?"

"That one."

A red laser light appeared where a hazy gray number was on one of the bottom boxes, and I strained to see it even more.

"What is i…" I turned my head at the same time as I spoke and stopped when I saw Max, a gun in his hand, aiming it at the screen.

My mouth fell open.

His eyes met mine, and he saw the way they were nearly popping out of my head, and then looked kind of sheepish.

"Fancy laser pointer you have there," I mused as he put the gun back in someplace behind his back.

Hmmm. I hadn't realized he was armed.

Imagine that.

"Sorry," he snorted. "Seemed easier than getting up. My knee fucking hurts."

"Everything always hurts," Jack agreed, retaking his seat.

These men were all older. Late forties, early fifties, I'd guess.

But, don't think for a second that these men weren't handsome as hell, or that they were any less dangerous than a younger man at his prime.

Nope, I'd been around my fair share of military men in my time. In fact, I'd been a member of the LTWC—Longview Texas Welcoming Committee—since I was a kid. Twelve at the most.

See, it all started when I realized how alone I really was in the world. Yes, I had grandparents, but they were literally all I had.

Which got me to thinking about other men and women who didn't have even what I had.

Then, one time I'd heard about a soldier coming home, and a welcoming committee was needed for him since he didn't have any family. So, I'd begged my grandmother to take me to Dallas, and together we'd welcomed home this young soldier from war. It was so satisfying seeing his smile directed toward us that I'd been doing it ever since.

In fact, I had one that I had to go welcome home in three days.

Most of these soldiers were young, but that made them no less deadly.

But these older men in the room with me, staring at me like I was amusing them, were definitely in their prime, right along with the soldiers I welcomed home every few weeks.

"I'll send it to my woman and see if she can do anything. She only has the laptop with her at work, though. It might take her longer."

Sam stood up and opened the door wide. "Janie!"

A woman whom I presumed was Janie came walking in with a sandwich in one hand, and a dill pickle in the other.

She was a gorgeous blonde with long, flowing hair, bright green eyes, and a smile that was stunning. She was slim on top, but her bottom half had a little more meat to it than the rest of her, making her hips flare wide.

"Yeah?" Janie asked, leaning forward to take a bite of her pickle.

It crunched noisily, and she looked sheepishly around the room, pausing only slightly on Rafe a little longer than the others, before returning her gaze to Sam.

"Can you do me a favor and bring me the report on a Drake Garwood?" he asked her. "Everything."

Janie nodded and turned to go.

I watched her hips sway as she walked away, and I wasn't the only one.

Rafe watched her, too.

Like a hawk.

But before Sam and the other two could notice, he returned his eyes forward.

And caught mine.

I raised my brows at him, and he gave me nothing in return. Not a smile. Not a shrug. Nothing.

Interesting.

Someone had the hots for the help!

Grinning, I went back to paying attention.

"In all honesty, I would've continued to keep my distance and only watched had I not witnessed that last night," Dante said, looking at the photos. "I have a feeling he's in it up to his eyeballs, and it won't be long before he's looking for alternate ways to get money."

"The info we pulled on Drake was bad if I remember correctly." Sam rubbed his forehead. "I can't remember exactly, though. I might be getting him and another guy mixed up. But I remember pulling her. She almost didn't make it. Wren, I think."

Jack grunted. "It was Wren. She was the one who showed up sick as a dog, battling a fever, and so banged up and bruised that we couldn't touch her anywhere without her crying out in pain."

Knowing that Marianne had gone through that was making me sick to my stomach.

"Only one of our birds who asked to go back, though," Max said. "That's why I remember her so clearly."

I had nothing to say to that.

Why would she go back if she was safe?

"They were exhuming the son's body, and they needed her eyewitness account to charge the husband," Janie said as she came into the room, looking down at the papers in her hands instead of at the room. She ran into a chair but didn't seem to care as she stopped and continued to speak as she read. "The case was almost dismissed due to not being able to find Marianne. According to Marianne/Wren, she went back because she wanted her husband to pay for killing her son. Only the case was dismissed anyway due to lack of evidence found during the autopsy, as well as the fact that Marianne had been diagnosed as clinically depressed at the time, which Drake's attorney used to get her testimony thrown out."

I remembered that vividly.

It'd been a huge case, and it'd also brought Marianne home. I'd been both stunned to see her and ecstatic that she was back. She seemed to be back to the old Marianne, that was until she'd started spewing all those accusations about Drake.

They'd been so outrageous that I'd not taken her seriously. How could I? The man that she described wasn't the man that *I* knew. *That anyone knew.*

Drake had never once shown himself to be anything other than a caring father and husband. He doted on their child, and he loved Marianne. He took care of her, and he supported her through her bout with postpartum depression.

Hadn't he?

Was I wrong? Had I gone against my friend, thinking that she wasn't in her right mind, only to find out that she had been right all along?

This was all so surreal that I was having a hard time making sense of it all, and I didn't know what to think.

"Marianne was diagnosed with severe postpartum depression," I found myself saying, my physical body in the room, but my mind had traveled back about two years into the past. "She told me once that she dreamed about killing her baby. Sending him to Heaven where he couldn't be hurt anymore."

The table quieted. "I always assumed that it was her, that it was because she… wasn't well. I never actually thought that any of it was true. The wild accusations and the way that she had acted… knowing what I know now… I just… well, I feel like I betrayed her as a friend."

God.

I hadn't believed her!

"Tell us about the times that you saw her. Was she always scared?"

Sam's quietly worded question had me nodding.

"I met her in the hospital when she had her baby, and we'd hit it off so well that we exchanged Facebook info. Shortly after that, we met for coffee. It just bloomed from there. But every time that Drake would come into the room when I was at their house, she would get all wonky."

"Define wonky," Sam ordered.

I bit the inside of my lip and closed my eyes as I recounted the first time that I wondered what was up with their relationship.

***

"This coffee is to die for," I exclaimed, inhaling the aroma that wafted from my cup. "I love it. I would totally box this up just so I could smell it. I'd probably get the same buzz from sniffing it as I would from drinking it."

Marianne started to laugh but that laughter quickly died when her husband, Drake, walked into the room.

I still wasn't sure what to think about that man.

He was handsome, in a polished sort of way. I normally found myself veering more toward the rugged, lumberjack type of men. Men with beards and longer hair, and who wore flannel shirts, work boots and faded jeans.

Drake Garwood was nothing like that, and I didn't think I'd ever seen him in anything less formal than dress slacks. Today he was wearing black suit pants, and a white long-sleeved, button-down shirt tucked into those pants. He finished it all off with a black belt, black dress shoes, and a burgundy tie. The suit jacket was slung over his arm.

He didn't smile when he saw Marianne. In fact, he looked at her almost… indifferently?

He didn't say anything as he went to the baby, Raymond, and picked him up out of his bouncer.

Marianne was practically quivering. But was it in anticipation or… something else?

I couldn't tell, but I definitely could feel the tension in the room. What was that all about?

I opened my mouth to say something, but the words froze in my throat when my eyes lit on the diaper explosion. Raymond had poop from the tops of his ears all the way to his feet. Only, before either Marianne or I could say anything, Drake curved his arm around the baby and cradled him close to his chest.

The bright brownish-yellow mess smeared the chest of Drake's shirt along with his hand.

Drake froze and then turned his angry gaze to Marianne.

"You let my child sit in this?" he snarled.

Marianne started to shake her head. "I didn't..."

Drake walked over to Marianne, thrust Raymond in her arms, covering her with the baby's mess, and then glared at her. Just when he was about to start yelling, my presence made his notice, and he hesitated.

"Clean him up."

Then he left.

"Marianne." I reached for the baby. "Oh God."

Marianne stood and then walked to the kitchen sink where she washed what she could off, then started emptying the sink of its dishes. Once she had that done, I walked over with the baby, and we set him down into the sink, hosing him off as best as we could with the sprayer.

"You're not seriously washing him in the sink, where our dishes go, are you?"

Marianne seemed to tense, her whole entire body freezing as she tried to say something that wasn't going to make him angrier but ended up not saying anything at all as she waited for him to continue.

"You are." He walked up to Marianne's side, this time in a dark gray shirt, and glared. "That's disgusting."

Marianne's lip quivered. "I'm sorry."

He didn't say another thing. He just walked straight out of the house without looking back.

"Ummm," I hesitated. "He does realize that babies are messy, right?"

Marianne shrugged. "I'm not all that sure that Drake actually knows anything at all about children."

***

"And, in all honesty, what he did that time wasn't all that worrisome. I think any man would've been upset about poop on their shirt before they went to work."

"No," Dante disagreed. "I'd give goddamn anything to have my child's poop on my shirt. Or their throw up. Hell, I'd give anything to walk into the laundry room to get one of my shirts only to find it stained with their crayons that got mixed up in the wash with my work shirts."

Nobody said anything.

"You have other kids?"

Dante made a sound in the back of his throat like a wounded animal. "No. Not anymore."

"I wouldn't be mad. Not like that," Max butted in, likely sensing the sudden tension. "I'd be peeved, but not at my wife, and certainly not at the kid. It's not like that's controllable."

I nodded, feeling weird all of a sudden. "I was a little weirded out by their interaction. But that was just one incident of many. Things like that happened a lot. I remember thinking that it was like he only picked their kid up for show, like he only did it out of obligation maybe. Marianne freaked out whenever he picked the baby up, almost as if she was just waiting for him to hurl the baby across the room. And that wasn't just once in a while—that was every single time that I witnessed it."

"Why did you think she had postpartum depression?" Jack asked. "What, other than what you've already told us, put all these red flags in your head?"

I tried to think back to an instance in time, and I couldn't pinpoint one.

"Mostly it was due to the fact that she said she had it, that Drake said she had it. Then, when the baby was younger, maybe about two months old, she told me about wanting him to go to Heaven. After that, it was like she almost stopped... loving him."

Dante hissed in a breath.

"What do you mean she stopped loving him?"

"The kisses," I said. "She used to give him kisses all day, every day. She'd dote on him. But, after she told me about that dream, it was as though she started to distance herself from him. I'd come over, and the baby would be crying. I'd arrive for coffee, and she'd hand him over, almost as if she couldn't get rid of him fast enough."

Nobody knew what to say to that.

"Maybe she was distancing herself because she knew he wouldn't be here much longer."

That was Janie.

We all looked in her direction.

"What?"

Janie flushed at Rafe's quiet question.

"Maybe she knew what was about to happen."

"You mean, maybe she knew that Drake would kill her child, and she was trying to minimalize her feelings so it didn't hurt as much?" I offered.

Janie looked at me and nodded gratefully. "Yes, exactly."

"Maybe," I murmured, looking down at my hands.

The room was silent after that, almost as if no one knew what to say.

"Well," Jack muttered. "I haven't heard back from Winter yet. Once I do, I can give you the number on those boxes... do you mind if I keep this?"

Dante waved his hand away.

"Fine."

Jack grunted his thank you, and I looked around.

Was this where we left? We didn't know anything more than when we arrived.

Well, kind of.

I now suspected that Drake was a terrible person who had a hand in killing my friend. She may not have died from anything that he could be convicted for, but he'd certainly played a part in how her treatments were handled.

Shit.

"Do I kick him out of my house?"

"I think you should tell him that you're selling it," Rafe piped in. "Tell him that you're strapped for cash and that you have no choice. If you want, I can be the go-between."

I looked at the man across the table.

"That makes sense," I muttered as I turned my eyes to the table, trying not to stare at the man.

Rafe—Raphael—was beautiful. So, so beautiful.

Normally, he would be the type of man I would go for. Tall, dark, and dangerous. But there was something about Dante, though, with his brooding good looks, and his anger that was almost palpable, that really had me gravitating toward him.

"If I tell him that I have to pay for cancer treatments, he'll understand," I muttered almost to myself.

The table went silent.

Sam, who was shuffling his papers into a neat stack, froze. Jack stopped repeatedly clicking his ballpoint pen. Janie, who'd been absently spinning in one of the chairs, stilled. And Max stopped tapping his fingers against the tabletop and stared at me.

Dante, who'd been at my side absently cracking his knuckles, was the only one who continued to do so.

My eyes came up, and I found myself staring at Rafe again, who looked considerably more interested in me.

"You have cancer?"

I opened my mouth to reply, but Dante beat me to it.

"Yeah, breast cancer. She says she's not doing anything for it, though."

I turned a glare on the man at my side.

They seriously didn't need to know that.

Rafe grunted.

I looked back at him, and he was scrutinizing me with a gaze that I was sure took in every minute detail, down to the tiny hairs that I probably had growing on my chin.

"I once thought I had testicular cancer, but it turns out it was an infection."

I blinked.

"You did?"

My eyes automatically went to his pants, where his testicles would be, causing him to laugh.

"If you're wondering, I lost one of the boys," he expounded.

"That's why we call him Uniball," Sam muttered, and he, too, was looking at me.

"Rafe will be a good fit for this, don't you think?" Jack asked, I assumed, Sam.

Rafe sat back in his chair and continued to study me.

"I have to go overseas in a few weeks, but other than that, I should be free," Rafe added.

Sam grunted and stood.

"Sounds like a plan." He handed the stack of papers back to Janie. When he'd taken them from her, I didn't know. "Make a copy of those and give the duplicates to Dante in case he needs what we have. Dante," he turned to study the man at my side, "when we get more info, I'll let you know. For now, Rafe is free to use as you please. If anybody asks, though, make it sound like you've hired him. We don't want anyone thinking he's working with us due to liability reasons."

Dante grunted. "Considering I'm already paying him..."

"I'm a Jack of all trades." Rafe laughed.

"You're a pain in the ass," Dante said as he stood. "Thanks for the help."

Then he shook all the hands in the room, including Janie's, but excluding Rafe's.

"I expect you to let my brother know that you weren't on the clock today," Dante grunted.

Rafe laughed then.

"I'll be sure to do that."

Then Rafe left.

"Janie, you got those papers?"

Janie jumped and turned to look at Sam guiltily. "Uhhh, yeah. Sorry. I'll get them right now."

Then she was gone, disappearing less quietly than Rafe had.

"Gonna be a problem."

I looked over to see Jack talking to Sam.

Sam grunted. "Don't start."

"It's gonna happen," Max said.

"What's gonna happen?"

All the men looked at me, and Sam grimaced. "Janie has a small crush."

No, Janie had a big crush. One that was going to get her in trouble, apparently. But, if I was a woman that looked like Janie, I'd have a crush on the bad guy, too.

"Hmm," I muttered, then smiled. "Thanks for helping us!"

I offered my hand to each man, and every single one of them squeezed it lightly, like they were afraid to break me.

I grimaced.

Yet another thing that I didn't like about having cancer. Once people knew you had it, they treated you differently.

Before, they might've just given me a handshake. Now they were looking at me like I was about to die any second.

Guess I had a whole lot more of that to look forward to, didn't I?

CHAPTER 9

*There are two kinds of people in this world.
Those who put their ketchup on the plate, and the
weirdos who squeeze it directly onto their fries.*

-Sincerely, Cobie, a fellow weirdo

Cobie

"I want you to make me a promise."

My brows rose as my hand stilled on the handle of the truck door. "What?"

My eyes met his, and I could practically feel the energy that he was trying to keep contained.

"I want you to call me if you think he's putting any pressure on you whatsoever."

I pursed my lips. "I don't think..."

He shook his head and held up his hand. "I don't live here. I have no clue if anything is wrong unless I come up here. You've already said you weren't leaving. You've also said that you're not giving up this house, and I understand that. Respect it even. But I have no way of knowing if you're in trouble if you don't tell me. Help me keep you safe."

I groaned. "Fine."

I pushed the door open, but he stopped me with a hand on my thigh.

I froze.

"One other thing."

I waited.

"Give the treatment a chance." I opened my mouth to say something, but he squeezed my thigh lightly, telling me without words that he wasn't through. "The world would be a lesser place without you in it."

***

Three days later

"The world would be a lesser place without you in it."

I replayed those words over and over again in my mind as I made my way into the office.

This place literally scared the crap out of me.

I'd spent some of the roughest months of my life here.

Cried here. Sweated. Cursed. Moaned and groaned.

This was also the place where I was set free again but where Marianne lost her battle.

Well, not at this exact office building, but this was the place where Dr. Todd told her that she wouldn't make it out of this alive. The same place that I'd left just a week ago, telling myself I'd never be back.

Yet, here I was.

The world would be a lesser place without you.

Dante's words replayed through my head during check-in as I played the waiting game in the waiting room, and all the way up until the moment when Dr. Todd came into the room.

He looked happy to see me, and I immediately felt like an ass for leaving the way I did last week.

"Cobie."

I gave Dr. Todd a smile.

"I'm glad you came back."

I shrugged. "I gotta be honest with you. I wasn't planning on it. But a friend gave me a few wise words, and I knew he wouldn't be okay if I didn't fight."

"Drake Garwood?"

I shook my head. "No. His name is Dante."

Then I blushed.

Dr. Todd smiled. "Like that, is it?"

I opened my mouth to deny it, but the words wouldn't come. Dr. Todd's smile widened.

I blushed harder.

He started to laugh, and I did, too.

He sobered a few moments later, and then he pulled out a computer, which he hooked up to a cord.

A picture of what I guessed was my breast flickered to life on the screen.

"Here's your left breast."

I nodded.

"This is the cancer. However, with as close as it is to this lymph node, we're going to offer two suggestions."

I listened as he explained what he thought I should do, and then I looked at my fingernails.

"You can do a lumpectomy, where we'd just remove the tumor and the surrounding tissue," Dr. Todd began. "Or, you can opt to do a modified radical mastectomy, which means we'd take the entire breast, including the nipple, the breast tissue, as well as the surrounding lymph nodes."

I swallowed.

"I agree with doing the radical mastectomy," I started. "But this could happen again, right? In the other breast?"

"Yes. Even if we do the full mastectomy on the first breast, there is a possibility that it'll recur in the other breast," he agreed. "But after we do the surgery and the chemo treatments, we'll keep an eye on it quite closely for the first year. After that, we'll monitor you with bi-yearly mammograms to keep an eye out for any changes, and I have hope that should it recur, we'll catch it early so it won't get to this stage again."

I didn't like that answer.

"Why not do both at the same time?"

Dr. Todd nodded his head. "Considering your history, this is an aggressive preventative course of action. Many patients in your shoes opt to go this route. Only you can make this call, though." He stood up and walked around the desk, leaning against it and crossing his feet in order to be closer to me. "There are other types of surgeries we can do where we leave the skin and the nipple in place, that way, later on when you have reconstructive surgery, it'll be more natural looking."

I grimaced.

I hadn't much thought about any of this.

"Is that more of a risk?"

"Anything is a risk." He hesitated. "But, there's less of a chance without the breast tissue there."

I let my eyes drift away from his, and come to a halt as I gazed out the window. The traffic was starting to get congested as the five o'clock hour hit.

People were heading home. Some to their families. Others to an empty home. *Like me.*

"What do we do first?" I asked. "When will this happen?"

He re-crossed his legs, this time with the opposite foot on top.

"We do it now. Your mammogram is recent enough to give us proper indication on where the cancerous tumor is," he said. "I'd want to do this soon. Maybe the beginning of next week so that it doesn't have a chance to grow or spread. Given your history with cancer, I really don't want to wait. On Friday, I'll send you to the hospital to have your blood drawn. If all comes back well with that, we'll schedule the surgery for Monday. Okay?"

I nodded my agreement.

Just the thought of doing this all alone again really fucking sucked.

"I need a doctor's note," I murmured. "I've missed a week of work, and I'm assuming I'll miss much more than that."

Dr. Todd didn't move.

"It's going to be all right, Cobie."

I just didn't see that right now, but maybe once it was all done and over, I would.

***

Four days later

"This is just a liability form." The registration clerk flipped to the next page.

Over the last four days, I'd filled out a total of eight million, seven hundred, and sixty-nine forms.

All of them were necessary.

After revamping my Last Will & Testament, taking Drake Garwood out of my will, creating a Living Will and finally changing over my life insurance beneficiary, this was nothing.

If I never saw a 'trust fund' or notarized document saying who I wanted my money to go to in the event of my death again, it'd be too soon.

I signed my name on the line where the clerk had indicated.

"This one is just in case you perish during the surgery. Your family won't be able to sue in your stead."

I almost laughed at that one.

"Okay," I muttered, signing that one without even looking at it.

"This one is in the event that we run into complications. You'll need to name the person who you'd like to make decisions for you in the event…"

I pulled out a copy of my Living Will.

"This will give you everything you need to know in the event of my incapacity," I said. "This also has a DNR—do not resuscitate—order attached to it should I become medically incapacitated, unless, of course, my medical power of attorney deems it necessary."

I thought long and hard about who to name as my medical power of attorney. It wasn't an easy decision.

Other than my co-workers, who, although bummed to hear that I had cancer and would be off for the foreseeable future, were not people I'd choose to have medical power of attorney over my life.

Then again, there was literally no one left.

With me being a homebody, there were only about five people in the world that I knew wouldn't freak out about being handed, essentially my life, on a silver platter. All five of them were people I'd known for about four days. And of the five, only one of them had been on my mind constantly over the last four days.

Dante.

Was this a weird request to ask of a man whom I'd only known for a few days? Yes. Did I have anybody else that I could ask? No.

And hopefully, he wouldn't even need to be advised of his new role in my life. Hopefully I came out of this surgery without any problems. I'd just wake up from the procedure with two less breasts, but a new will to live.

Hopefully… hopefully, Dante never needed to know who he was to me until I was no longer of this Earth.

"Excellent," the woman who was partially responsible for my numb hand exclaimed. "That negates these three forms then."

My hand thanked her.

"Okay, the last one is this. Consenting to the surgical procedure itself."

I rolled my eyes as I sloppily scribbled my name, and then pursed my lips and offered her the last page.

"All right, have a seat in the waiting room, and you'll be called back soon."

I did as she asked, took my seat, and waited for the next step with my heart in my throat.

I continued to rethink my decisions, but each time I did, Dante's words would replay in my mind.

The world would be a lesser place without you.

The world would be a lesser place without you.

The world would be a lesser place without you.

And, as the nurse placed the mask over my face and told me to breathe deeply, the cocktail of drugs pouring through my veins, the last thought I had before the blackness took me was that maybe Dante didn't know me well enough to make that statement. *Maybe the world wouldn't even notice if I was gone.*

CHAPTER 10

*You got in trouble for saying crap? That's not a
fucking swear word!*

-Dante to his eight-year-old niece.

Dante

I walked into the office, and the first person I saw was my brother.

He looked at me like I'd grown a second head.

"What are you doing here?" he asked, looking as dumbfounded as he sounded.

"I own this shit hole," I muttered, passing him by without slowing.

"Can I hold her?"

I paused, turned, and then hesitated.

Travis narrowed his eyes.

I handed Mary over, and then turned and walked away.

If I stopped, then I'd have to go back and take her away from him.

It was hard for me to give her up. In fact, the only person I'd willingly given her to at this point was Krisney, my brother Reed's soon-to-be wife, and that was it.

Krisney and I had kept up some over the years since she and Reed had broken up, and when they'd gotten back together, I'd found that she was one of the only people who I didn't feel threatened by.

Why that was, I didn't know, but it was what it was.

I couldn't help my irrational fears.

In reality, I knew that my brothers wouldn't do my daughter any harm. Then again, when I'd sent my children and wife with my sister, Amy, that day, I hadn't thought that she was going to kill them, either.

Jaw clenched, I pushed the door to my office open and winced when I saw it exactly as I'd left it.

Had Travis been in here at all since I'd left?

"I haven't been in here at all since you left. I didn't want to touch anything."

I looked around the office. At the stacks of papers on my desk. The picture frames that Lily had put there our last Christmas together, replacing the older, outdated pictures with the newer ones. Hell, even a coffee cup, one that proclaimed me a 'Papa Bear' still sat on the edge of the desk. That, and there was dust fuckin' everywhere.

"I can have the cleaning lady clean if you want."

I swallowed.

"Yeah," I croaked. "I think that would be good."

I took a step into the room, and the first thing I saw was the wall of fuckin' pictures.

Lily loved pictures.

She loved them so much, in fact, that she put a cork board wall up in my office. Then, when she found the time, she had hundreds of pictures developed. Each picture would somehow find their way to the wall.

The entire wall was covered in mine and Lily's life.

Our children.

Travis and his daughter.

All of my brothers.

My parents.

Lily's best friend, Ruthie.

I rubbed my chest absently when one picture, in particular, hurt a little too much to see. A photo of my girls and Amy, laughing as they painted their nails.

"I..." Travis stopped when I wiped my eye. "Dante..."

I cleared my throat. "I'm not going to hide anymore."

Travis didn't reply.

"I'm sorry for putting you into the position that I did," I told him, still studying the wall. "I don't know that I figured out what to do yet, but I'm going to try."

Travis's hand came down on my shoulder.

"Dante, we all understood," he growled. "We all understood, and we all are here for you, no matter what you decide. Hannah picked up a lot of the slack, and honestly, at this point, you're just icing on the cake."

Pretty much, I was no longer needed. Travis had taken over with his new wife, Hannah, taking over for what Lily and I used to do. Where Travis had been the extra hand in the background, now that was me. The place that Lily and I built together was no longer ours, and instead, it was theirs.

But I'd done that to myself.

By disappearing when my wife and children had died, I'd essentially forced Travis to make that decision. I'd made him do something he'd never wanted to do, and for that, I'd have to deal.

A loud smack of skin against skin had my head turning in the direction of my daughter and Travis.

Mary reared back and then struck the palm of her hand against her uncle's hand once again.

"She's beautiful, D."

I studied my daughter and agreed wholeheartedly.

"She saved me."

Travis's eyes met mine. "I know. And she'll never know this, but I thank the lucky stars every single night for her bringing you back to us."

Before I could reply, though, my phone rang.

I reached for it, never too far from it since the accident, even if I never answered all of the calls.

Placing the phone against my ear, I answered with a short, "Hello?"

"Mr. Hail?"

I frowned.

"Yes?"

"This is Risa Carver, a nurse at the Medical Plaza in Longview?"

I frowned. "Yeah?"

Travis caught Mary's hand in his and studied me as I listened.

"I'm calling to let you know about Cobie?"

My entire world froze.

"Is she… is she okay?"

God, if she died, I'd feel fuckin' terrible.

I'd thought about nothing but her over the last four days, which had prompted my trip into the office. I needed something to take my mind off of the woman, and appease the guilt that I was feeling.

Guilt that never went away.

Lily, my wife, was dead.

And I'd only made promises to her for when she was alive. But my heart didn't agree with that.

That time that I'd slept with Marianne… it'd been a fuckin' crazy night.

I'd been drinking. Marianne had been drinking. It'd gotten quickly out of hand.

The next morning when I'd woken up in her bed with the mother of all hangovers, the guilt had set in.

I'd slept with another woman who wasn't my wife for the first time in almost ten years.

And now, my mind was so occupied with everything Cobie that I could barely function.

"Oh," the nurse apologized. "Cobie is perfectly fine. It's just routine that we call about halfway through surgery to let loved ones know that the surgery is going okay."

"Surgery?"

I sounded like a goddamned parrot.

"Yes, Cobie's surgery that started at seven this morning?" the nurse said. "The double mastectomy?"

Double Mastectomy. What. The. *Fuck?*

She was having surgery?

"Oh, yes," I lied. "Do they expect her out of surgery soon?"

"She has another four hours or so, they presume. You have plenty of time."

Plenty of time for what?

"I just wanted you to know how she was doing. If anything happens between now and when they're done, I'll be sure to let you know."

"Okay, thank you for calling."

And then she was gone, leaving me standing there, the phone still to my ear, looking at my wall of pictures as my mind raced.

"Who was that?" Travis asked worriedly. "Surgery? What surgery? Is someone having surgery?"

I held my hand up to calm Travis's worries. "No one you know."

"No one I know?" he parroted. "But *I* know everyone *you* know."

My brows rose, and I started to chuckle. "Not this girl."

"Girl?"

My eyes met his, and once again I saw the look of shock on his face.

"Girl," I confirmed. "Woman. She's got cancer. I met her... I met her a few days ago."

It would be too hard to explain to him why I knew this girl. And honestly, I didn't feel like explaining anything more to him than I already did.

"You met a girl who has cancer a few days ago, she's having surgery today, and they called you?" He looked confused. "If you just met her, why would they be calling you?"

That was a good question. Yet, I somehow knew why they were calling me.

Most likely, she'd put me down as an emergency contact thinking they wouldn't call me at all. Wasn't that usually what happened? But I knew for a fact she wouldn't have put me down if she thought they were going to call me just for an update.

"Guess that's a good question," I muttered, taking one more glance around the room. Taking a deep breath, I turned my back on the wall of pictures and the emotion that was bubbling up inside of me and walked toward my brother. "We're gonna go."

Travis held onto Mary when I went to remove her from his arms. "I'll keep her. I know you're going to go. And a hospital is no place for a toddler to be."

I didn't know what to say.

On one hand, he was right. A hospital was a terrible place for a toddler. Hell, my office was a terrible place for Mary to be. Yet, I couldn't quite make myself let go. She'd been my saving grace. My hail Mary. The idea of leaving her with Travis had a cold sweat blooming all over my body.

"I swear," Travis said, reading my mood. "I'd never, not ever, put her in any danger."

I swallowed, then took a step back.

Travis watched me. "Give her a kiss, man."

Those words sent me into a tailspin. A memory slammed into me so hard that I gasped in a breath.

***

"Give her a kiss, man," Travis growled. "We gotta go!"

I grinned and turned to my wife, who was bent over, strapping our kids into my sister's car.

93

I walked up behind her and smacked her on the ass, laughing when she yelped and turned.

I caught her head before she could slam it on the roof of the car, and she glowered at me.

"I'm sorry," I lied. "I don't know how that happened."

She snorted, then turned to finish buckling Toni into her car seat even though Toni had been able to do it herself for a while now. At her age, she was well on her way to doing a lot of things on her own. Her momma still doted on her. Then again, her daddy did, too.

Toni was my girl. My mini-me. The little bit of a girl who would always love her daddy more than her mommy.

Which sucked for Lily. Me, not so much.

I walked forward until my hips were pressed against Lily's backside, and pulled her back by her hips so that she could feel the erection that was clearly evident.

"You're terrible," she muttered, backing up.

I let her come, and then grinned when she turned around and wrapped her arms around my neck. "I'm terrible," I agreed. "But sometimes I just can't help myself."

Lily grinned, her bright eyes shining with happiness. "I love you, Dan-Dan."

I snorted at her pet name for me and wrapped her up tightly. "I'll be back late. Don't wait up for me."

She returned the kiss, and then I let her go before pushing her to the side and leaning into the car. "Y'all be good for Mommy tonight, do you hear?"

"Yes, Daddy," both girls said like the angels they were.

I snorted. "Love ya!"

Both girls blew me kisses, and I backed out of the car, turning around to see Lily staring at where my ass had once been.

"Now which of us is terrible?"

Lily grinned. "I didn't smack your ass, which is more than I can say for you."

I snorted and smacked her ass again as I started to walk away.

"I love you, Dan-Dan!"

I waved at her over my shoulder and took the shotgun seat in Travis's truck.

"Let's go."

We pulled away before Amy had even gotten behind the wheel of the car, and she waved as we made our way out of the parking lot.

Travis and I waved back, passing over the huge bridge that spanned the length of the river.

My eyes went down, and I grinned over at Travis. "We should go fishing. With the river up like it is, the trees won't stop us from going downstream."

Travis grunted. "What does it matter? The last time we went fishing in that river, you made me get out and wade over the fallen trees. Even when you said the same damn thing that time, too."

I chuckled, then sat back in my seat and closed my eyes.

The river was completely forgotten as I thought about all the paperwork that we were going to have to do for this recovery.

It was going to be a long damn day.

* * *

"D?"

I swallowed and looked up to find not just Travis in the room, but Rafe, Evander, and Parker—another new hire—there as well.

Parker and Rafe had been working there for a while now, but this was my first time actually meeting Parker.

And what I saw in his eyes matched mine.

He'd lost someone, too.

Fuck.

We both looked away from the other's pain, and I turned to Travis. "If you're sure about keeping her, I would like you to hang on to her. I don't know how long I'll be, though."

Travis hitched Mary up higher onto his hip, and then walked forward and waited.

I dropped a kiss to Mary's forehead, once again wishing I could kiss my other two babies one more time, and headed out the door without another word to anyone there.

CHAPTER 11

I used to be like you, all smiley and shit.

-Cobie's secret thoughts

Cobie

My eyes opened, and the first thing I saw was the white ceiling. The next thing I saw was the bright white IV pole at my bedside.

The next thing I became aware of was when I let my eyes trail down the length of the IV pole, hesitating slightly at the monitor that was there before they continued on down until something else caught my eye.

My mouth fell open.

Then the pain made itself known, and I moaned.

Dante, who was at my bedside sitting straight up in his chair but asleep, shot up like I'd stabbed him in the thigh.

"Cobie?"

The concern in his voice had my eyes filling with tears—though that might've been due to the pain as well. I wasn't really sure at that point.

"What are you doing here?" I croaked.

And what the hell? My chest felt like it was on fire.

"I…." He looked at me in concern. "Are you okay?"

I tried to nod my head yes but it came out as a moan. "It hurts."

He curled my hand around something, and then said, "This is the pain pump. They explained it to you when they brought you in from recovery, do you remember?"

No, no, I didn't remember a damn thing. The last thing I remembered was having my breasts drawn on with a magic marker.

I couldn't function for a few minutes as the pain started to consume me. What felt like an hour later, awareness slowly started to seep back into my brain, and I opened my eyes that I was unaware I'd closed.

"Better?"

I swallowed, then croaked, "Yeah."

He looked like he was about to pull his hair out.

"Good."

I must've looked confused, because he gave me a half-assed smile as he said, "I'm here because they called me to let me know how you were doing about halfway through your surgery."

My brows lifted. "Ummm," I hesitated. "They weren't supposed to call you at all."

He nodded. "I had a feeling that was what happened. But I'm here now. For another hour or so, anyway. Mary goes to bed around seven, and I left her with my brother."

I didn't know what to say to that.

So, I said nothing.

"I'm glad you decided to fight."

I opened my mouth to reply, but decided nothing I could say was going to matter at this point.

I was fighting…but maybe not as hard as I could've been.

***

Eight days later

"All right," the nurse who'd just redressed my chest said. "If you need anything at all, please don't hesitate to call. The next doctor visit has already been scheduled, right?"

I nodded.

"Okay, good. Do you know what you need to do from here?"

I nodded again.

"Great."

I looked at all the flowers from my co-workers that dotted the ledges of my hospital room.

The only bouquet of flowers that was delivered personally was the small wildflower mix that was in a hastily-grabbed Texaco cup—and those were from Dante.

The rest were from my co-workers, and for the most part, I was happy that they hadn't totally forgotten about me. But neither did they take the time over the last few days to come and see how I was doing. That kind of hurt, especially since I was only one floor below them. It wouldn't have taken them much time at all to come to my room for a quick visit, but none of them had done so.

Which was for the best, I guess.

If they'd have come, then I would've had to talk to them.

Talking to them at work was hard enough. Talking to them after I'd had surgery? Yeah, that would've been torture.

"The only ones I want are in that Texaco cup." I indicated to the wildflowers, and the nurse went and got them, handing them to me.

I carefully reached forward, realizing rather quickly after my surgery that sudden movements weren't my friends, and settled the cup on my lap.

They weren't much. In fact, they looked like they were picked off the side of the road, but they meant the most to me.

I'd never gotten flowers before. Not like this, where they actually meant something to me.

Using the pillow that the hospital gave me to clutch to my no-longer-existing breasts, I gripped the cup and looked at my lap as the nurse pushed me down to the lower level.

"I never thought to ask," the nurse hesitated. "But you do have a ride, correct?"

I winced. The reason they'd kept me in the hospital as long as they had was because I didn't have anyone to help me at home. And, since they had the open room, the doctor had ordered me to stay.

However, today they'd deemed me well enough to navigate the world on my own. Lucky me.

I nodded at the nurse but didn't make eye contact. "I do."

The taxi was bright yellow and front and center as we passed through the double doors.

"The taxi." I indicated where I wanted to go.

The nurse frowned. "Do you have help?"

I wanted to laugh at that.

I hadn't had help in so long that I probably wouldn't know what to do with it if I did have it.

"Yep," I lied. "They're stuck at the airport, though. They'll be meeting me at home."

The lie felt bitter on my tongue, and I wanted to growl in annoyance at myself.

I hated lying. It never solved anything.

Except for this one time, anyway.

"Okay," the nurse replied skeptically. "Let me know if you need help. I'm sure we can find you someone."

Yeah, right.

I ignored her offer of help, even though I probably shouldn't have, but I was determined to do it all myself.

I was ready to freakin' cry after just getting myself settled in the cab.

By the time I got home and through my front door, the pain was washing over me in waves and I could feel the tears pooling in my eyes.

I spent the next hour in the foyer, sitting on the bench, as I tried to gather the strength I'd need to move to the kitchen so I could take a pain pill.

At least I'd thought ahead and had the hospital fill it for me.

Thank God.

The thought of doing anything other than lying there on the foyer bench was a foreign phenomenon to me. I decided that I'd just lay there for a little bit until the pain eased enough for me to make my way to the kitchen.

Once it kicked it, well, then I'd attempt to make it up the stairs.

I slowly laid myself down, one millimeter at a time until I was fully on my back, closed my eyes, and prayed for the pain to calm.

CHAPTER 12

Live slow, die whenever.

-Tattoo

Dante

Later that afternoon

"What do you mean she's gone?"

"She was released earlier this afternoon, about an hour ago, actually," the nurse who'd taken my call replied. "Did she not tell you?"

No, she didn't tell me. Otherwise, I likely would've been there to pick her up, you dumbass!

Instead of saying what I was thinking aloud, I thanked her and hung up.

Then I looked over at Mary. "You want to go for a ride?"

Mary was always up for a ride.

Her smile told me so.

Forty-five minutes later I arrived in front of her house to find her car in her driveway, Drake's car behind it and him waiting at the front door.

I drove on past her house and circled around the back side of the neighborhood, coming up the back alleyway like I had the last time Drake had been in her driveway.

Mary was sound asleep as I pulled her out of her seat, and she didn't wake but for a moment as I readjusted her onto my shoulder.

I looked at the old house that belonged to Cobie and studied the rocks outside.

Kicking over the closest ones with my foot, I was disappointed to find there wasn't a key like there'd been the last time.

I smiled. *Good girl.*

The next place I checked was under the mat, then the eave above the door.

No key.

I tried the door handle.

Locked.

Shit.

My eyes trailed over to the window directly next to the door, and on a whim, I tried it.

Stuck.

The window opened a millimeter and screeched to a halt. *Shit.*

Doing this one handed also wasn't helping. But, with a little determination and strength, I was able to shimmy the window open far enough to reach my hand around for the doorknob.

I'd have to rectify that problem once I got inside. I was sure since the thing was barely moving that she thought it was safe to leave it alone, but it wasn't.

After popping the lock on the door from the inside, I opened it from the outside and walked in.

The kitchen I walked into was stifling.

It felt hotter inside than it was outside.

I frowned and closed the door behind me, locking it moments after that.

Drake was still knocking on the front door, but I ignored it as I made my way through the kitchen.

That'd been as far as I'd gotten the last time I was here, so I was a little surprised when it spat me out into a formal dining room, followed next by what I assumed was the living room.

The wood on the floor creaked underneath my feet, groaning every now and then when I stepped on a particularly weak piece.

Passing by a couch that looked to be one of the most comfortable I'd ever seen, I kicked the footrest up and laid the chair back, depositing Mary. Once she was safely on the couch, I snatched the old quilt off the back of the couch and covered her up with it. But only partially. With it being as hot in here as it was, she'd kick it off if it was covering her too much.

She was like me in that way. I always hated to be hot when I was sleeping. It was the best way to ensure that the sleep would be the worst I'd ever had.

Then again, I'd found something that caused me to sleep even less than being hot did…but I couldn't find a way to fix a broken heart.

I hadn't slept much since the accident. Maybe, if I was lucky, a couple hours a night here and there.

Now I lived off of maybe two or three hours, and I was lucky if I got that.

The knock at the front door started up again, and I wanted nothing more than to yank the door open and tell the stupid man to fuck off.

If she hadn't answered it by now, she wasn't going to.

The knocking had me walking toward the front door instead of upstairs as I'd intended, and I froze when the door came into touching distance.

Why, you ask?

Because Cobie was on her back on the most uncomfortable looking bench I'd ever seen in my life, crying silent tears.

"Cobie." I dropped down to my knee beside her. "Fuck, are you okay?"

She managed a pitiful moan that would've brought me to my knees if I hadn't already been there.

"It hurts so bad," she whispered. "I hate the pain. It sucks."

Her ragged breathing had me feeling like the most unfeeling person in the world.

"Did they give you some pain meds?"

She licked her lips. "They're in my pocket."

Her pocket?

I reached forward, patting her pockets.

She was wearing scrubs, likely ones she'd received from the hospital, and the pill bottle was tucked into the first pocket I came to.

I took the bottle in hand, walked away from her even though it was hard as hell to do, and to the kitchen where I got her a glass of water.

Once I had that, I shook out one pill, put the rest on the counter for later, and went back to her.

She was still there, silently crying.

"Can you sit up?"

She shook her head, and the movement shook the ponytail loose of the half-assed up-do that she had it in. It fell down around her face, making my stomach clench.

I ignored the urge to touch it, to wind it up in my fist, and worked my arm underneath her.

Once she was sitting up, fresh tears streaming down her face, I placed the pill against her mouth.

She opened it, tried to swallow it dry, and then moaned when it got stuck at the back of her throat.

I placed the cup to her mouth and tilted it for her to drink, and she drank it greedily.

She was about halfway done when she lifted her chin, pushing the cup away without words.

"Do you want to sit here for a little bit? Want me to carry you to the couch? I'll do whatever you want."

She inhaled deeply.

"I think if you move me, it'll hurt too much."

She panted some more, and I felt so fuckin' helpless. I wanted to punch the damn wall behind her head.

I hated seeing people in pain.

I hated feeling helpless like this, like I was an inadequate loser who could do nothing right.

"I think that you're already in pain," I said softly. "Let me move you to the couch. This has to be uncomfortable."

She looked at me, tears still leaking out of her eyes, and then nodded once.

I didn't hesitate.

I picked her up, gently, and moved her to the couch.

A woman hadn't been in my arms like this since my wife died, and I had to say that the feeling wasn't altogether unwelcome.

Sure, I'd slept with one other woman—Marianne. But that had been nothing but me being drunk, and touching her as minimally as possible to get the job—a release—done. I knew before it was even over that it was a mistake, yet I'd continued with what I'd started because Marianne seemed to be enjoying it. She had no way of knowing that it hadn't been the same for me.

That I'd been blaming and berating myself nearly the entire time.

Even in my drunken state, I'd worn a condom, and that had been something I hadn't had to do for a very long, long time. Lily had been my college sweetheart, and I'd had one other person in my life before her. That had been the one and only time I'd used a condom in as long as I could remember. I was surprised I even remembered how to put one on seeing as it'd been so long and how incredibly drunk I was.

A squeak came from Cobie, and I froze in my attempt to put her down.

"Can you just… wait."

She was suspended in the air, half down, half up—her breathing ragged as she pinched her eyes closed. The tears still leaked out, though. Each one breaking my heart more and more.

I picked her back up, and she dropped her head to my chest.

"Can you do this for just another minute?"

Hold her in my arms?

I could probably do it all day long if she asked me to.

"What about if I sit?" I asked.

Then I'd be able to hold her a lot longer.

"I don't know," she admitted. "Try it, and I'll let you know."

I slowly sat down on the couch, holding her in my arms, cradled like a small child to my chest.

My eyes went over to where Mary was still sleeping, having kicked the blanket off even more, and something in my heart settled.

There, on the couch, with Mary sleeping next to my thigh, her tiny feet touching my hip and Cobie in my arms, her tears slowing... I found peace for the first time in years.

***

Cobie

Awareness of something other than pain came to me in slow, aching increments.

The first thing I saw was Dante's throat, which was dripping sweat.

I pulled my head away from said throat, and looked at his face, only to see his eyes closed.

His breathing was even and deep, letting me know that he was asleep.

I smiled, turned my head, and gasped.

His little girl was sitting up on the couch, her eyes on me.

I smiled, and she smiled back instantly.

It was the most beautiful thing I'd ever seen.

"Hi," I croaked.

She leaned forward and started to crawl toward me, but stopped when she reached her father's side—my side.

Her hand went to my foot, and she touched my painted red toes.

I'd gotten a pedicure before I'd gone in for surgery, and it was apparent that Dante's girl approved.

"Pretty?" I asked her.

I tried to move, but the pain made itself known again as a sudden stab of pain flashed through my chest.

Okay. No movements whatsoever. Got it.

"Her name is Mary."

I looked slowly back over to Dante and smiled when I saw his eyes on me.

"She's gorgeous," I whispered.

But I could tell with just one look that this little girl wouldn't be like all the other girls.

Mary had Down Syndrome.

Her eyes were canted up and slightly close together.

Dante seemed to know what I was thinking and opened his mouth.

"I didn't know she had Down Syndrome until I took her to the pediatrician for a well-check a few days after Marianne brought her to me," Dante said, holding out his hand for his daughter.

She took his hand, wrapping both fists around one finger, and brought it up to her mouth.

She pressed a slobbery kiss on it, and my heart melted right then and there.

"Does she have heart problems?"

Normally one of the downsides of having Down Syndrome was heart problems—CHD. Congenital heart disease, to be specific. I'd spent quite a bit of time during nursing school working on a floor where one of the patients seemed to have rented a room there. He was always there, and over time, I got to learn a lot about him and the problems he faced.

Over the six months of that particular semester, Dobbie (his real name was Corrone, but the kid loved him some Harry Potter) had been one of my patients. Each time I'd have a clinical, that little boy would be there. I watched him struggle. I watched him succeed. I watched him get released. Then I watched him come back and go through it all over again. Finally, after about four months of being in and out of the hospital, he got to go home for good.

And now, years later, I was still in touch with their family. I went to Dobbie's birthday parties, he turned six this year, and I also got to go to his pre-school and kindergarten graduations.

"No," Dante murmured. "Doctor said, as of right now, that she has a clean bill of health. He did say that she might run into problems later on down the road, but we'll jump those hurdles when we get to them."

I took a deep breath, and my eyes closed as the pinch of pain struck me.

"I have to use the bathroom," I murmured. "And I know you have to be tired of holding me."

He grunted something but stood up as if I weighed nothing and started up the stairs. "There's a bathroom down here."

"Is your room down here?" He paused with his foot on the first step.

I shook my head. "No."

"Then we'll go to this one so you can change your clothes."

I wanted to change my clothes. I also wanted to change my underwear, but I wouldn't be telling him that. In fact, he wouldn't be helping me change my clothes, either.

Before I could inform him of that, though, he walked me straight into my room—which was the first door we got to—and headed to the bathroom that was in between my room and the next room.

"How did you know this was mine?"

"Only door open," he answered, flipping the light switch on. "Do you need help doing this?"

I was about to say no when he gently placed me on my feet.

My knees were wobbly, and I made a noise in my throat that he took as a sign that he was going to stay and help me.

"Dante…"

"Hush," he growled. "I've helped my share of girls and women use the bathroom in my time."

I didn't know what to say to that.

With one hand around my hips, he plucked the string on my pants and then started to shove them down my legs.

"Please," I said. "I barely know you, and I want to try to do it myself."

He paused, looking up at me from his hunched over position. "Do you have anyone else to help you?"

I opened my mouth to reply but quickly shut it.

"That's what I thought."

Then he shoved my pants down my legs.

I was then, officially and thoroughly, overwhelmed.

Before I could so much as moan in embarrassment, though, he helped me sit, and then walked out moments later.

I sat there for a few seconds, completely pitiful, before I did my business.

My panties were the only thing I could manage to get up, and even those were a struggle.

He came back moments after I got them in place, and then helped me walk to the sink.

"Do you want to wash your face or anything?"

"What's wrong with my face?"

My startled question had him grinning. "Nothing. Just figured you were a girl, and you've been in the hospital for the last eight days. Wasn't sure how much cleaning you got done."

I had nothing to say to that.

"A sponge bath courtesy of the aide," I mumbled. "I'd love to wipe it down, though. Amongst other things."

He nodded and looked around, spotting the washcloths that were on the shelf above the toilet. Grabbing three, he turned on the sink and started to run hot water. Once he had it where he wanted it, he pulled the stopper up and blocked off the drain, allowing it to fill.

About the time that he would've turned it off, we both heard a very loud, "Da!"

Dante grinned. "Be right back."

He was gone seconds later, and I heard him plodding down the stairs, then his happy voice saying, "Hey, girl."

I turned off the water and stared at myself in the mirror.

I'd never have that. I'd never have a kid to call my own. One who I would talk to like I'd missed her for however long she'd been asleep. I wouldn't be able to have kids. Not with this cancer crap I had. I couldn't trust that I'd live long enough to make it through the majority of my kid's life.

With shaky hands, I dunked the cloths into the sink and then reached for the pump soap.

Just as I'd gotten two squirts into the water, Dante reappeared, with Mary in his arms.

My heart completely melted, and I straightened…then immediately regretted it.

Tears burned my eyes as I took a deep breath, which also fuckin' hurt.

I remained still as I closed my eyes and waited for the wave of pain to recede.

"You have two more hours until you can take any more meds," he said apologetically. "But I can help you get cleaned up."

I nodded, swallowed thickly, and then opened my eyes.

Dante sat Mary on the floor, then turned around and closed the door.

Mary immediately went to the toilet, and Dante closed it. "No, ma'am."

Mary gave him a look that said she was clearly not pleased with his refusal to allow her to play in the toilet.

"Here."

Then Dante handed her his phone, and I watched in amazement as she opened it, pulled up her favorite app, and then started to play.

"Wow," I breathed. "She's better than me."

Dante chuckled as he walked up to me. "The girl is pretty damn amazing."

I smiled softly and reached for the wet cloth that was submerged in the sink.

"I'll do it." He stilled my hand. "Let's get the shirt off first, though."

Before I could protest—again—he had the buttons halfway undone.

Loss so great it was debilitating had me speaking up this time, though.

"I don't…" I started to shiver. "I don't want to look!"

He paused.

I could see the gauze that was wrapped around my chest, and I really, really didn't want to see anymore.

"Close your eyes," he ordered as he moved me to sit on the counter.

I did, unable to help the fear that poured through me, and gave myself that out.

He could look if it meant that I didn't have to.

I knew that eventually I'd have to, but the time for me to do that wasn't right now.

Maybe tomorrow or the next day, but I just didn't have it in me today.

The shirt came off the rest of the way, and he gingerly removed it from my arms, keeping my movements as shallow and slow as he could make them.

He did the rest of the work, gently pulling it over my head and tossing it somewhere on the floor.

I could hear the beeps and blips from Mary's phone, and I opened my eyes to look at her, being sure not to look down.

"I don't see Marianne in her at all," I whispered.

Dante grunted. "Looks just like my kiddos used to."

A pang of sadness washed over me at the knowledge that this man in front of me had lost his children. I wished I knew more, but to know more, I'd have to ask him. I wasn't sure asking him was the right thing to do. It was obvious that it was still raw, so I chose not to say anything about his other children. Instead, I focused on Mary and Marianne.

"Marianne's other son, the one who died, looked nothing like Marianne, either. It was funny because I always used to joke with her that the hospital had switched the baby at birth with hers. He had dark brown hair, steel blue eyes, and shared absolutely none of her features. Though, he also didn't look much like Drake, either."

Dante grunted, but did nothing more than that, leaving me to wonder if I should continue with my observations.

"What was Marianne like?" Dante surprised me by asking.

I smiled. "Kind. Loving. Devoted to her son. Which always surprised me with the postpartum depression thing. I never saw her being distant with him. Never saw her do a single thing that would've set off alarms inside *my* head. She was utterly devoted to him."

Which made me feel a little guilty.

"I should've questioned the depression. I just never thought to. She was the one who told me that she had it. Who was I to argue with that?"

"You couldn't," he said. "My wife had it with our kids for two or three months. It was so weird. She just wouldn't have anything to do with them. She let me do all the heavy lifting, so to speak. Diaper changes. Getting up with them in the middle of the night. Baths. Then, one day, it was like she was back. Boom. She was the devoted mother again. Though, that was due in part to her doctor prescribing her meds to help battle it. Once she took them, she was better. But, you would've never known, on the outside, that she had it. My wife—she hid it and played the part for everyone but me. Why *would* you know? If someone says that they have something, who am I or you to tell them that they don't have that?"

116

I was glad that she had that with him. *Wasn't I?*

I wanted so badly to ask him about his wife. Where was she? Would she care that this man—*her man*—was currently taking a washcloth to a practically naked woman? I would, even if all he was doing was helping.

"Well," I hesitated. "I didn't notice it. That's just my opinion."

"Do these drains need to be emptied?"

The drains in question were there to help release the fluid from inside my chest. In a week or so they'd be removed, but for now, they were my new friends.

"Yeah," I cleared my throat. "Please."

"How?"

So, there I sat, half naked, telling this man how to empty the drains that were pulling fluid out of my chest cavity.

If this man wasn't already married, I just might have to hug him.

"That kid of yours," I murmured as he emptied the second drain into the sink. "She's good. I've watched her beat three levels at that game she's playing."

He looked over and down at her, grinning slightly. "My other daughters used to love that game. Really all you do is touch the shape. Pretty simple, but it helps them learn the name of the shapes as they do it since it calls it out. Though, there's one shape—circle—that sounds more like 'jerkyll' to me."

I would've laughed, but the inhalation I took in order to expel the laughter wound up stealing the breath from my chest.

"Don't laugh," Dante said as he saw my face.

I didn't have anything to say to that, mostly because I couldn't.

I just nodded, closed my eyes tightly and started to count to a hundred in my head. I got to thirty before the pain began to ebb. Forty-nine when it became manageable enough to open my eyes again. It was at eighty when I felt that I could speak without crying.

"That wasn't good," I wheezed.

Dante didn't say anything as he finished up his work and then left the room.

I waited, knowing he had a purpose and wouldn't forget me, and wasn't disappointed.

He came back with a button-up flannel shirt.

One that I knew wasn't mine because it was about eighteen sizes too big.

"Where'd you get that?" I questioned, looking at the fabric with a curious eye.

"My truck."

My brows rose.

I hadn't heard the front door open and told him as much.

"I parked in the back," he said. "Your friend Drake was at the front."

My lip lifted in a silent snarl. "He called me. I didn't answer."

"Why?" Dante asked as he laid the shirt on the counter, and then lifted another washcloth out of the sink.

This one he ran against the exposed skin of my neck and belly. The last one that was in there he used to wipe down my face.

"I've never felt something so wonderful in all my life," I told him.

He grunted. "Showers make everything seem a lot more bearable."

I agreed with that wholeheartedly. I could be having a really shitty day, and all I would need to do was go take a shower, and it didn't seem as bad by the time I got out.

Then again, the one-hundred-and fifteen-degree water that I used to shower with likely fried away some of my working brain cells.

"All done," he said, causing me to look up at him.

I watched as he moved me where he wanted me, drying me off and placing his shirt on my body.

I observed him, taking in everything about him that I could. He had blond hair that was short on the sides and spiky on the top. But I doubted that he put gel in his hair to keep it spiky like some men did.

His eyes were blue and so freakin' clear that they reminded me of something out of a storybook. Or maybe a Disney movie. His eyes were impossibly hard not to stare at.

Then there was his chest.

Dante wasn't lacking in the muscles department. He had a lot of them. I could see them through his white T-shirt—and did I mention that a white t-shirt and jeans were my absolute favorite thing ever on a man? Because they were. And on Dante they were perfection.

I could see his nipples.

I could *see* his nipples!

Dear, sweet baby Jesus!

"You want to go to your bed or back downstairs?"

I blinked, coming out of my contemplations of his various assets, and pursed my lips in thought. "I think I'd like to sit on the couch. When I was in the hospital, it hurt way worse to be lying flat on my back rather than propped up in the bed."

Dante nodded, his eyes contemplative as he looked down at Mary.

"Let me take her down first so she doesn't try to follow us, and then I'll come back for you."

I stayed where he put me while he did just that, and wondered if I should ask him to leave.

He'd done a lot for me. Surely, he was ready to go.

I was positive that he had stayed way longer than he'd intended, and when I told him so moments later as he arrived back in the bathroom for me, he looked at me incredulously.

"I'm not leaving you here alone the day you get home from the hospital where you had a surgery that left you in tremendous pain, weak and barely able to walk."

I snapped my mouth shut.

"I don't want you to feel like you have to stay if you don't want to," I started again.

"For now, I'm exactly where I want to be," he informed me. "Now, let's go. We have about two hours or so before we have to head home."

I did as he asked. Then again, I didn't have much of a choice in the matter seeing as he'd picked me up and carried me downstairs.

**

Dante

Two and a half hours later, I bundled up both Mary and Cobie— who was good and drugged up on her pain medication once again—and got them settled in my truck.

Cobie had given me a half-hearted reply of 'yes' when I'd asked her if she wanted to come to my house, and I drove us all home.

Both Cobie and Mary slept the entire way there, leaving me to my thoughts.

And they definitely weren't good.

At first, all I could think about was that Cobie was sitting in Lily's spot. Then, it was how Cobie was going to be staying in Lily's and my house and how I wouldn't be able to just get rid of her if a freak out started.

Minutes after pulling into my driveway—the one that was just down the road from my brothers' houses—I moved before I had time to think.

I got Mary first, and instead of putting her on the floor, I laid her on the couch.

She'd been a love/snuggle bug for hours today with Cobie, and she was sleeping just as much as Cobie was, which was abnormal for her.

Then again, there wasn't really a 'norm' when it came to toddlers. They did what they wanted and always would.

After making sure Mary was comfortable on the couch, I went back outside for Cobie and carried her into my home as well. The guilt immediately hit me as soon as we crossed the threshold.

I didn't see Mary as a betrayal to my wife's memory. She was a baby, my baby. Lily would have expected me to care for her, to bring her home.

But carrying another woman into our home and sitting her in my wife's favorite spot? Yeah, that felt very much like a betrayal to Lily's memory. It burned as I swallowed the bile down.

CHAPTER 13

Stupid people are like glow sticks. I want to bend
them in half until they break, and then shake the
shit out of them until their light turns on.

-Cobie's secret thoughts

Cobie

I woke up hurting, but not nearly as bad as I'd been hurting when I got home yesterday. Then again, that had a lot to do with the fact that Dante forced the meds down my throat, whether I was awake or not.

The first time he woke me in the night, I was disoriented. I didn't know where I was. I wasn't sure who was standing over me, nor what was going on. But, slowly my eyes had focused.

I quickly realized where I was and who exactly was standing over me.

The second time he woke me, it was close to six in the morning and I had a lot more going for me. I not only knew my name, but also where I was and who was in the room with me right away.

Then he told me he was leaving, and I smiled and thanked him for all the help.

Only now that I was fully awake and more with the program, I realized that earlier when I thought I'd known where I was, I was mistaken. I wasn't in my bedroom. I was in a bedroom that looked kind of like mine, but it wasn't actually mine at all. For starters, the door was in the wrong place, and I'd never seen the comforter that was covering me before in my life.

Painfully, I made my way to a semi-seated position—and I only made it to the semi-upright position because I couldn't lift myself up all the way without shooting pains stabbing me in the chest.

Settling for this partially hunched position, I started to make an attempt at standing but paused when I heard footsteps.

I stopped mid-stand and took a seat on the bed, waiting with anticipation for the door to open.

It did open, but the person on the other side wasn't anyone I'd ever seen before.

"Oh!" the very cute blonde woman exclaimed. "I didn't know you'd be awake yet! Dante said you'd probably sleep for another few hours. I was just bringing you your phone and a bell."

I must've looked confused because she grinned.

"My name is Hannah." She waved, smiling brightly. "My husband is Dante's brother."

"Hi," I croaked.

Hannah grinned at me. "I'm a nurse. Or I used to be. Well, I guess that I always will be. My license is still up to date, but I mainly work with my husband as well as Dante now that he's back. I'm so glad he's back, by the way. When Travis called me this morning to ask me if I'd help, I jumped at the chance. He's the only brother out of all of them who literally has nothing to do with anyone. It's sad."

I blinked at that information overload.

"I'm a nurse, too," was the only thing I could think of to say.

Hannah laughed. "Sweet! We're going to get along famously, I just know it!"

Then she walked forward, rubbing her hands together, almost as if she was getting ready to start in on a discussion that would take hours.

I had to stop her.

The urge that woke me in the first place made itself known again, and suddenly I was very glad that Hannah was here and not Dante.

"Not to be rude, but can you point me in the direction of the restroom?"

"The potty is down the hall," she pointed, then blushed. "I have three young kids. Potty seems to be my go-to word. Sorry."

I huffed a small laugh and stood, this time all the way up, and started to shuffle forward.

"I'm a fall risk," I told Hannah. "But I'd like to go to the bathroom by myself if you don't mind."

Hannah stayed at my side but didn't try to grab hold of me, and I was thankful. Dante helping me felt a lot different than some stranger. And, frankly, I wanted to do it myself. I wanted to feel like myself again.

Yesterday when I'd left, the nurse that gave me my discharge paperwork had told me to keep on top of my pain meds and try to walk as much as I could tolerate.

And thanks to Dante, I'd done very little walking. Not that I was complaining, but I wouldn't have him there forever.

Eventually, I'd have to do these things on my own, and it would probably be sooner rather than later.

Dante didn't strike me as the type who would tolerate me being in his space for too long. He might have been nice to me out of obligation yesterday, but I wouldn't take advantage of his kindness. That just wasn't me.

And I'd survived a lot of stuff on my own. I could do this, too.

Plus, I was fairly sure that his wife wouldn't appreciate me being here.

Which made me wonder, where was here? And would she be showing up anytime soon?

"This is the bathroom," Hannah pointed. "Those two doors are locked. I think they're the kids' bedrooms, but I'm not certain. Dante's bedroom is at the end of the hall. That one is Mary's."

As she pointed out the rooms, I tried to memorize what she was telling me, but I realized rather quickly that I didn't really need to know what rooms were where. As soon as I could get my next dose of pain meds, I was going back home. I couldn't be here. I couldn't be indebted to anyone.

Not even the sweet, sexy man, Dante.

This was my cross to bear, and I'd do it on my own. That much I knew for sure.

Was I thankful for his help yesterday? *Hell yeah.* Was I going to allow it for any longer? *Hell no.*

I'd screwed up by not staying ahead of my pain yesterday. But you could bet your ass I wouldn't be making that same mistake again.

Why, you ask, was I so stubborn?

Because nobody does anything out of the goodness of their heart. Nobody.

Everyone has a price. Everyone has a reason for doing what they do. And I had a feeling that Dante's reason was because he felt guilty and sorry for me.

I was nobody's problem but my own.

Hannah pushed open the door to the bathroom, then gestured me inside.

"Do I happen to have any clothes?"

Hannah nodded her head. "Your bag is downstairs. Do you want it?"

I refrained from saying something smart like, I wouldn't have asked if I hadn't wanted it.

Instead, I tilted my head once. "Yes, please."

She was gone a few moments later, and I waited for her to come back up with my clothes before I started anything.

She was back within moments, setting the bag on the counter. "I can help you get ready when you get done using the bathroom."

Yeah, right.

I smiled, but didn't disagree nor agree with her. I didn't lie. Lies had a way of getting you caught up in stuff you wouldn't normally have been involved in. So, I tried not to go that route if possible. It was just as easy to smile and stay silent as it was to say a lie anyway.

She was gone before I could say anything more, and I was grateful that she didn't try to linger. The urge to pee was almost unbearable now that I was within seeing distance of the toilet.

Heading to the commode using small, shuffling steps, I did my business. Long minutes later—because nothing was easy, even using the bathroom—I was back up, this time standing in front of the mirror.

Time to face the music.

Letting Dante's shirt fall from my body, which took a hell of a lot longer than I would've wanted, I stared at the gauze.

It was innocent, really. Until you thought about what it was concealing. Only then did my heart start to slam. To literally pound in my chest.

I swallowed and started to unravel it.

The minute I saw what remained of my chest, a little squeak of air left me.

I closed my eyes and started to cry.

***

Dante

"Ummm, Dante?"

"Yeah?"

"Is there a way into the bathroom that doesn't involve me breaking the door down?"

I paused with my sandwich halfway to my mouth, and said, "Why?"

"Because your friend went in there over an hour ago and hasn't come back out. When I call her name, she doesn't say a thing except for 'be out in a minute.' She's said 'be out in a minute' at least fifteen times to me. It's time for her pain meds, but I can't get her to open the door."

I looked over at Mary, who was asleep in the playpen that was set up in the corner of the room, and then down at my sandwich.

Figuring I could finish it on my way, I said, "I'll be there in a minute."

Then I hung up before she could say anything else.

After taking one more look at Mary, I walked out of my office, and into my brother's. "Will you watch Mary for a half hour? I have a problem at my house."

Travis held up his thumb but didn't verbally answer. "No, our company doesn't like doing those kinds of pickups because they're dangerous."

I rolled my eyes.

I was glad that I'd been on the phone, otherwise Travis would've let me answer it, like he'd been doing lately.

Apparently, he was 'all answered out' as he liked to say. Though, I didn't blame him. It'd been entirely way too long since I'd answered a single phone call. I could see why he would want a break.

Which was also why I didn't complain. Not one single bit.

I owed him quite a lot, and an apology was definitely among the things I owed him. Yet I couldn't seem to get the words out.

Like this morning, when I'd called to ask him if Hannah would be willing to spend the day at my place helping Cobie, I could've offered him that apology then, but I didn't.

Couldn't, really.

I was a coward.

"Thanks."

Then I walked out the office door, down into the forecourt of Hail Auto Recovery, waved at my brother, Baylor, who was pulling up with his own truck, and kept right on going.

Baylor hollered my name, but I waved at him and said, "I'll be right back."

Baylor nodded and shut the truck off, his eyes watchful.

He didn't believe me.

Hell, all of them watched me with a look of uncertainty, as if they didn't know if I was going to be there from one minute to the next.

Then again, I couldn't say that I blamed them. I spent two fuckin' years in my own head, and for one of those years, I hadn't spoken to them at all.

The other year, I'd only surfaced if one of them was hurt, which made me a pretty shitty brother if you asked me.

Their calls had been among the ones that I'd ignored, multiple times. Hell, multiple wasn't even an accurate description to cover how many times I'd ducked one of their calls. If I had to guess, it was hundreds, maybe even thousands, of calls that had gone unanswered by me. Ninety-nine percent of them had been from my brothers.

As I drove to my house, the one that I'd once shared with Lily, I contemplated what I'd do once I got there.

I had a way into the bathroom, but that way required me to climb up the back side of the house and enter through the window. A window that was locked, but I knew how to jiggle it just right to get it open—something I'd found out after Lily and I had locked ourselves out of the house one too many times.

First, I'd try to get her to open the door the normal way, and if that didn't work, then I'd do the climb and hope I didn't die thing.

But after knocking on the bathroom door for a few minutes without a reply while Hannah looked on worriedly, I chose option two. Partly because I didn't want to mess up the door. It was an antique that Lily had lovingly restored. It was tattered from years of abuse before we'd gotten it, and she brought it back to life. I couldn't break it down—I just didn't have it in me.

So, with no other choice, I walked around the back of the house and looked up at the window on the second floor.

This hadn't been easy the other times I'd done it, but with a bit of elbow grease and some determination, I was able to hoist myself up and over the ledge of the house.

I managed to get all the way to the top before I looked down, and doing that made me wince, which had to be why I didn't bother actually looking into the bathroom through the window until I had already jimmied it open and was shoving my body through the way-too-small window.

And when I finally did look up at her, I completely froze in my tracks.

I sat on the window ledge, eyes glued to the woman standing in front of the mirror. Tears were streaming down her face and trailing all the way down her naked torso, over her belly and soaking her panty line.

"Do you think," she whispered. "That it would be inappropriate for me to go topless at the beach?"

I thought about the question before I shrugged. "Probably not inappropriate, no. But I do believe that people will stare. If you don't want them to stare, then I'd cover it up."

I hopped down from the window, trying my level best to not look at her body, but…I failed. I also didn't know what the protocol was when it came to staring at a mostly naked woman who had just undergone a double mastectomy.

Should I avert my eyes? Should I stare at her and act like I wasn't doing anything wrong? Pretend that there wasn't anything missing?

I don't know what the damn protocol is for this kind of stuff.

"It looks and feels weird," she whispered, lifting her hand and pointing at what I was trying valiantly *not* to look at. "I was a thirty-six C before. I didn't have big boobs, but they weren't small, either. They were normal boobs, but now, they're just…not there anymore."

I stared at her breasts, or what was left of them, anyway. And there wasn't much. Not really. Mainly just the painful looking scars where her breasts used to be.

The drains that were coming out of each side of her chest wall were drawing more of my attention, and I couldn't help walking up to her side and reaching for the drain that was well on its way to half full.

I'd never actually done anything like this before. The only medical-type things I had ever done had been while I was in the military, and they had been more trauma related. Lately—just last week in fact—I'd had to put a Band-Aid on Mary's newly skinned knee.

She didn't move a muscle as she watched me perform my newly acquired skills, and I kept glancing up at her face, wondering if she was going to say anything.

She didn't disappoint me, only it wasn't what I expected to hear her say.

I thought she might've come out and said that this was incredibly awkward, which it was. Or maybe that she was hurting, which I could tell was happening beneath her carefully void exterior.

But what she said instead was, "I'm going to go home today, and I don't want you to feel bad when I do."

I blinked.

"Why?"

"Why what?"

"Why are you going home?" I asked. "You didn't ask me to bring you here. I decided to bring you here on my own. If I had a problem with you being here, I would've left you at your place, and called in a few favors to get people to check on you."

She looked away from my face and down to her scars again.

"Nobody does something for nothing."

Her murmured words had my brows raising.

"No," I agreed. "Not usually. And in this case, you'd probably be right. But I don't feel right about leaving you all alone at your place when I have nobody here in mine and the ability to take care of you."

"I don't want to be anyone's burden." She kept speaking in such a low, broken tone that it nearly hurt to hear. "I'm tired of being that person."

I didn't know what to say to that, but I felt her words in my soul.

"My family died in a car accident," I told her. "My wife, two children, and my sister were in the car. My sister was driving, and she was high on pain pills at the time. She was the only one who survived. I had to listen to them die while I was on the phone with them."

Her eyes widened in shock.

Mine did, too.

I couldn't believe I'd told her. I couldn't believe that I was able to get the words out.

Normally, they got stuck in my throat. I would try to get the words out, to voice the devastating truth, but it was almost as if my body would physically stop me from talking about it. As if I didn't say it, then maybe it wouldn't be true.

It'd been years, and it still felt like it had happened yesterday.

The wound from losing my family was still fresh, and it would forever be a gaping one. It still bled. It felt like I was still in shock most days, and I sometimes wondered if it was really as bad as it sounded.

But this reality of mine was really that bad.

Each morning I'd pray that it was all a bad dream.

Each morning I woke up, and my wife and kids weren't there.

They didn't run to me when I emerged from my bedroom, and my cycle in this living hell would start all over again.

God, it fucking hurt.

It hurt so goddamned bad sometimes that I could barely draw a breath.

But then Mary happened.

She saved me.

Every day that she was there since she'd been put into my care by her mother was a day that was a bit less bleak than the day before it.

I wouldn't say that the life I lived was a good one. I was basically just surviving on the hope that someday it might not hurt as much as it did now. Maybe one day, just the thought of my kids no longer being here to come running into my room and bounce on my chest each morning wouldn't hurt this much. But that day wasn't anywhere in sight for me yet, and I had doubts that it ever would be.

"I'm sorry."

I looked up to find her eyes on me.

"There's nobody here that'll complain about you being here. I'm trying to get back into the swing of working, and a lot of shit has piled up during the years that I hid my head in the sand. I'm needed at work, and Travis, my brother, deserves the break. The house is big. It's empty, and it's quiet. Honestly, you'll be doing me a favor by staying."

She looked torn. "You don't even know me."

I shrugged. "You don't know me, either."

A little smile kicked up at the corner of her lip. "True."

With nothing else to do but hope that she would come to the decision to stay on her own, I offered my shower to her.

"You want to shower?" I questioned.

"I can't," she hesitated. "They said not to get the incision wet until they take the drains out at the one-week follow-up."

I nodded my head. "That doesn't mean we can't do the bottom half."

My phone rang before I could do anything more, and I held up a finger and said, "Give me a sec."

She nodded her head and slumped even more forward, causing me to worry.

I answered it at the same time that I walked to the door.

"Yeah?"

"We got problems," Travis said.

My heart started to slam inside my chest, and every possible horrible scenario started to play through my brain. My hand froze on the doorknob, and it took everything I had not to drop to my suddenly shaking knees.

"What?" I croaked.

Travis cursed. "It's nothing bad. Not with Mary, anyway."

Relief poured through me, and my vision went momentarily white.

"Fuck."

"God, I'm sorry," Travis said. "She's still sleeping in your office. I just went and checked on her. But I got a call out, and I have to take it because everyone else is otherwise occupied. Drake's truck broke down right outside of town, and I need to go get him. Mom's here, and she wants to take Mary home with her."

I opened my mouth to immediately deny it, but the denial stuck in my throat.

"She says she'll even take her to your house."

Then the words that he'd said before pierced through my freak-out fog. "What is Drake doing in town?"

Travis grunted. "I don't know. Reed called me to tell me that he needed assistance. Since I'm a nice big brother, I said I'd do this one favor for him."

Thoughts started to flit around in my brain, and I cleared my throat. "I have to talk to you about something later. Can you come over when you're done?"

"Yeah," Travis said hesitantly. "What do you want me to tell Mom?"

"Tell Mom to take Mary to her house," I answered. "And I'll come get her later. I still have some work to do, but I'm going to help Cobie get cleaned up and then hand her back over to Hannah."

Travis grunted something. "You want me to meet you at the office or at your place?"

"Office," I answered.

I needed to talk to Rafe, and I needed to talk to Reed to figure out why Drake was here. It didn't seem like a coincidence that I took Cobie out of her home, away from him, and now he was here. Coincidences were never really coincidences when they came to men like Drake.

I just needed to know how he'd figured out that she was gone and how he knew that she'd gone with me.

But I didn't want to alarm Cobie while I did that.

"10-4," he grunted. "I'll tell Mom. I think you might've just made her day."

Then he hung up, leaving me with a sick feeling in the bottom of my stomach. One that was a combination of worry, anger, and sorrow.

"Is everything okay?"

"Yeah," I grunted, then opened the door.

When I did, I found Hannah on her butt across the hallway as she played on her phone. Upon me opening the door, she stood up and smiled hesitantly. "Everything okay?"

I nodded. "Can you go grab her pills for me?"

Hannah rushed off to do that, and I made a mental note to thank her later. She didn't know me all that well, but she hadn't hesitated at all when I asked her to come up here and take care of Cobie.

I appreciated that greatly.

I turned around and gestured to the shower. "There's a seat in there you can use. Just sit down on it, and I'll get Hannah to help you wash. Is that okay?"

Cobie nodded her head hesitantly.

"Are you okay with me leaving to go back to work again?"

She nodded again.

"Hannah's getting your pain pill. It was due about twenty minutes ago, so I have a feeling that you're going to start hurting any minute now. While you still can, I'd suggest getting in there and doing your thing. Do you like tacos?"

Cobie flicked her head and then nodded once.

"Good," I started to laugh. "Because other than gas station chicken, that's all there is here. I'll pick up some tacos on the way home. If you can think of anything else you need, let me know, okay?"

She swallowed.

"You'll be here when I get back?"

"Yes."

There was no hesitation in her voice, and something inside my chest that I hadn't realized was tight loosened. "Good."

Then I was gone, passing Hannah in the hallway. "Get her cleaned up if you can. She said she can't get the incision wet, but she'd enjoy a bath if you can figure out a way to do that without her getting those wet."

Hannah smiled. "I think we can manage."

Then she was gone, leaving me in my hallway, staring at two women interact in my bathroom. In Lily's favorite room of the house.

"I miss you, Lil," I said to the open air.

Nothing happened. Nobody responded.

And that pit at the bottom of my belly grew another inch.

CHAPTER 14

You're going to basic bitch hell.

-Cobie to Dante when he proclaims he doesn't like pumpkin spice

Dante

Three days later

I was going to let her do this without me, mostly because she'd specifically requested that I stay away. But the fear that was in her eyes as she made her way up the steps of the hospital had me parking the truck and following her inside.

I honestly didn't think she'd intended for me to see that change in her demeanor. But the moment she'd thought I was out of sight, I'd seen that fear take over her entire being. She was deathly afraid of what she was going to hear when she went into that office.

She hadn't wanted me to see the fear. In fact, she'd almost been a robot this past week.

It was as if she was trying really, really hard not to appear needy.

And I respected that, but it was also quite frustrating.

All I wanted to do was make sure that she was okay. Offer her a friendship.

Sure, at first, it'd been about the promise that Marianne had requested of me.

But then I'd gotten to know her.

This past week she'd definitely grown on me.

We'd both been hesitant when I'd come home that first night after seeing her newly acquired scars.

She didn't know what to say to me, and I didn't know what to say to her to make it all better.

I wasn't sure that it could get better.

Hell, I knew that my situation would never be better.

But her situation, well, it could get better. She would overcome this. She would be stronger and better able to function at the end of this without the threat of impending doom hanging over her head.

Shaking off my morose thoughts, I parked the truck in a lot intended for doctors, not giving that first fuck if I took some doctor's parking spot because there wasn't another towing company around to tow me, and mine wouldn't tow their own company's vehicle. However, I'm sure that the hospital wouldn't be amused that a towing company refused to come get it. And before they could call anybody else—which would have to be an eighteen-wheeler wrecker, seeing as my truck was so big and heavy—we'd be done in the hospital.

Grinning for the first time that day at the thought of pissing somebody off, I made my way inside.

I had to ask the receptionist which floor oncology—the cancer doc—was on. Once she directed me, I studiously avoided the place that I remembered going with Lily to. Doctor's appointments and well-checks for our children.

I didn't use the same pediatrician for Mary that we did for the other two kids.

140

Another doctor had recommended that I take her to see a doctor in Longview, a full hour away from where my other kiddos' doctor was located, because he specialized in cases like Mary's.

Not that Mary was a hard case. There were hundreds of thousands of people in this world with that extra chromosome that caused Down Syndrome. They had jobs. They lived normal lives. They got married.

Thinking of all the things that the doctor had shared with me when I'd first taken Mary to him, I made my way to where the aide had pointed me, arriving at the oncology doc's door within two minutes.

I spotted Cobie across the room, head down, staring at her knees.

Not stopping to question why the hell I was there in the first place, I strolled across the room and then dropped down into the seat beside her.

She looked up, startled by a person sitting down next to her in a room full of empty chairs, and closed her eyes. The relief on her face was enough to make me decide to stay whether she asked me to leave her alone or not.

"Dante…"

I winked and leaned over to pull out my phone. "Figured it's just as easy to sit in here as it is to sit out in the parking lot. At least this way I'm not wasting diesel."

Cobie smirked and looked back down at her knees, then pulled out her own phone.

So that was how the next five minutes went as we waited for the doctor to call her back. Most of the time was spent showing each other funny memes. Mine came from my brothers. Cobie's came from the internet.

I had never had, nor would I ever have, a Facebook account. I wasn't all that interested in the world knowing so much about me. If someone wanted to chat or say hi, they damn well knew my phone number. And if they didn't know, then they could come find me.

It wasn't like I'd left town.

My house, yes. Town, no.

The cabin was nestled deep in the woods of Hostel, Texas located along the same river that had stolen everything from me.

"Look at this one."

I grinned when I read it. Just a random question that an author who Cobie followed had asked.

Do identical twins have the same size penises?

"I'll bet that identical twins aren't identical everywhere. I used to know a few when I was in the military. Two of them were in the same unit as me. One was tall and slender while the other was just as tall but a bit stockier. Oh, and that Brock guy who works for Travis and me? The one who stopped by last night to bring me some paperwork? That guy's a twin, too. You should ask him."

She immediately shook her head, a smile creeping up over her face.

Brock was a good man, as far as I could tell. He was always on time. He always showed up for work, and in the brief time since I'd returned to work at Hail Auto Recovery, he'd been a stellar employee. My brother had done well hiring him.

However, when he'd arrived last night, his eyes had gone directly to Cobie who was situated on the couch, her eyes on the TV. She'd been snuggling with my daughter, both of them engrossed in a show that had been on ABC Family.

Brock took one look at her, and his whole demeanor had changed.

He'd gone from looking lazy to alert, and it hadn't taken a genius to see that he'd found her attractive.

I didn't like the way he looked at her last night, and twelve hours later, I still didn't like it.

But, as with all things that were starting to make me feel again, I buried those thoughts deep and locked them behind a door that I wouldn't be opening. Not ever.

So, in order to ignore the way that I was still mad about Brock staring at her, even as innocently as he had, I went back to reading on my phone.

I'd been doing that a lot over the last two years. I read before Lily had died, but now with those long sleepless nights, I had to do something to fill the time. Physical exercise only lasted so long— and my body wasn't that of a twenty-something-year-old man anymore. I was forty-one. I couldn't do the all-day workout thing anymore, or I'd be physically unable to walk.

Hence the reading.

"Whatcha readin'?"

I looked over to find her staring at me expectantly. "Jim Butcher."

"Jim Butcher is the title of the book or the author?"

"Author," I answered distractedly.

"What does this author write about?"

I grinned and looked over at her. "Paranormal and science fiction."

Her eyes widened. "I like that."

I rolled my eyes. "You can sign into my Kindle account and read them. I started this series for a second time, but I have all of them."

Greedily she signed out of her account and into mine, and soon I got her started on the first book in Jim Butcher's *Codex of Alera* series.

She was an entire two chapters in before she was called back, and without her asking, I got up and followed her in.

The doctor was waiting on us when we arrived at the exam room, and he smiled warmly at Cobie.

"Cobie, come in, come in."

"Hi, Dr. Todd." She shuffled slowly, careful not to make any sudden movements that would cause her pain. "This is Dante. He's my shadow."

Dr. Todd grinned. "I'm happy to hear that you have a shadow, Cobie. Hello, Dante. I'm Holman Todd."

I shook the man's hand, and he gestured for me to follow Cobie into the exam room, who was already taking a seat on the bench.

"How is everything feeling?"

"You mean, does it feel like I had my boobs chopped off?"

I winced.

Dr. Todd snorted. "Well, I assumed it would feel like that seeing as you did, in fact, have them removed."

I couldn't help but smile at that, and Cobie couldn't, either.

But her smile fell, and she stared at the doctor intently. "Let's talk about what you found."

Dr. Todd didn't dally. He pulled out the file that was on the corner of the counter, placed it into his lap, then reached for his reading glasses that were in his front coat pocket.

Placing them on his nose, he stared at Cobie over the rims. "We were able to get all of the cancer."

Both Cobie and I both breathed out roughly.

"How do you know?" I found myself asking.

He glanced over at me.

"Our hope when we went in there was to determine how much of the tissue was affected by the tumor," the doctor began. "It's always a worry that when we begin the surgery that the affected area could have spread to the chest wall, or the muscles surrounding the breast. However, in Cobie's case, the cancer was limited to the breast tissue itself. We were able to remove all of the affected area, as well as the surrounding tissue completely. The cancer also didn't spread to the lymph nodes, either."

I knew that was good. Cancer spreading to the lymph nodes meant spreading to the rest of the body. And spreading to the rest of the body was also what would kill her.

"But when she spoke about having it, she said that she'd be dead at the end of the year if it wasn't treated," I found myself continuing. "Does she have to have any further treatments aside from what she's already done?"

"Follow-up," he answered. "We're going to be doing regular tests on her to make sure that the cancer is no longer there. That's a simple blood test. At that time, we'll determine if a final round of chemo will be needed—which they usually do anyway, just to be safe. She'll get those blood tests quite frequently until I'm well satisfied that she has nothing else to worry about."

I clenched my jaw, then released it.

Cobie cleared her throat delicately.

"What now?"

Dr. Todd smiled. "Now you live your life."

Thirty minutes later, after removing the drains, we were walking slowly out the door.

I'd offered to get Cobie a wheelchair, but she was bound and determined to walk out of the hospital.

I let her, but the entire time I stayed with her, step for step, stopping when she stopped.

What would've taken me two minutes or less to do, it took her ten. But she made it out of the hospital on her own two legs, and then I convinced her to allow me to bring the truck around—thank God.

Watching her struggle was enough to make my heart hurt.

Cobie was a strong, independent person. Something that I'd learned very well over the last week that she'd been with me at my house. She hated having things done for her and would much rather do them herself.

I knew for a fact that she would rather be at her own house, suffering in silence.

But for some reason, I couldn't let her go.

Each day that she'd come up with an argument, I'd have a better reason for her not to go.

We'd done this quite a few times, the back and forth thing. I knew what was coming when she got to the car, but I thwarted her words by asking a question of my own, first.

"You want to try to get something to eat?"

Her eyes went up to me. "Sure, but didn't you say that you had to go get Mary from your mom?"

I nodded. "I figured we'd go get her first, then head to somewhere small and light. It being already two, I'm not going to want to eat all that much or I won't be hungry for dinner. Regardless of whether I am or not, Mary always is. So, since she has to eat, I like to cook her something, even if it is just frozen chicken and rice or something similar to that."

Her smile was soft. "I think I'd like to try to eat."

***

An hour later, we were in the middle of the restaurant named 'Sweet Tea.' Sweet Tea was a restaurant that catered to folks who liked good, old-fashioned, home-cooked meals. They also had some of the most amazing sweet tea I'd ever tried.

And that was saying something because I'd commit murder for some sweet tea from McAlister's or Chick-Fil-A. Sweet Tea, though? Yeah, they got the top spot, and I guess they should with a name like they had.

"Have you ever been here before?"

I nodded. "I like to come here when I have to take Mary to her doctor appointments," I answered. "Plus, with it being smaller, not as many people will come here. Then again, I'm convinced that's only because not that many people know it's back here. It's hidden in this little nook." I indicated to the shopping center that Sweet Tea was located behind.

The shopping center was popular, but the street behind it was rarely used because there was nothing beyond it. Nothing but the most hidden gem in the entirety of Longview, Texas.

"Do you want a booth or a table?" The hostess smiled at us, her face bouncing between me and Mary, to where Cobie was standing only a few inches away.

She was standing so close because the trip to the hospital wore her out, and she was trying not to fall to the floor. At one point on the way across the parking lot, I put my arm around her and held her to me. She'd gratefully taken the support, but she had straightened back up once we'd arrived inside.

I also refused to be saddened that I no longer felt her body weight in the curve of my arm or acknowledge the fact that I missed it.

I looked around the room and pointed to the booth in the back. "Can we have that one?"

It was in the corner, with windows on all sides, meaning Mary likely wouldn't get bored.

But ever since I'd picked her up from my mom's she'd done nothing but sleep. By the looks of her, tired and blinking sleepily, she'd likely not be able to make it through dinner.

I frowned.

Had she not slept while at my mom's?

Thinking about Mary and not about who was in the diner, I'd almost made it all the way to the table before I looked up and realized that the person we were sitting next to was none other than the man who we were all supposed to be avoiding—Drake.

Cobie hadn't noticed him yet, but oh, Drake had noticed us. And what I saw on his face was not a look of excitement.

If looks could kill, I'd be dust.

"Sorry, but would you mind putting us in that one over there?" I asked. "The sun is hurting my eyes over here."

My murmured words to the hostess had her turning and smiling.

Even at forty-one years old, I still had it.

Not that I wanted it.

But at times, it was useful.

Like now.

Drake glared at me as I passed, and I tilted my head down once in acknowledgment.

He didn't return the gesture…not that I'd expected him to.

Shit.

I thought about leaving, and honestly, I was ready to say to Cobie that we should go, when she exhaustedly collapsed into the chair and looked at me like she was ready to break.

"When we get back, I'm taking a four-hour nap."

I tightened my lips and sat down next to her, not wanting Drake at my back.

She looked at me curiously but otherwise didn't say anything about me sitting on the same side of the booth as her.

With the new position, Mary curled her head into my neck but reached out to offer her hand to Cobie, who took that hand and brought it up to her lips.

"Such a sweet girl," Cobie cooed.

Mary held onto her hand and didn't let go, as she breathed into my neck and went limp. Back out like a light.

My eyes, however, were glued on the man turned almost around backward in his booth, staring daggers at us.

I averted my eyes in order not to incite him into coming over, and said, "Drake's here."

Cobie started to look around, but I growled at her. "Don't."

She froze, her eyes on me, and said, "I thought you said he was in Hostel?"

I shrugged. "He was."

At least, that's the last time I'd known his actual whereabouts. I hadn't thought to keep up with him this week once I'd known that he was in town visiting family—oh, and that his truck was in our shop getting fixed.

I'd asked to be told once it was fixed, and I hadn't heard anything to the contrary.

Except, apparently, he was gone and in Longview again—eating at the same freakin' place that I'd decided to take Cobie *and* Mary to for lunch. Just freakin' perfect.

Two people that I knew would stick under his craw.

Sweet.

"Oh, shit," Cobie muttered. "What now?"

I didn't know.

"I guess we eat and try to act like we don't notice that he's angry," I suggested. "If we were to get up and leave, I think it'd be a little more suspicious."

"It'll probably be suspicious if I don't say anything to him. I do know him, after all."

"Just act like you didn't see him, and it'll be okay," I muttered.

Mary twitched in her sleep, and I repositioned her until she was laying on my other side, making it easier for her to sleep, as well as Cobie to continue holding her hand.

So, there we sat, speaking about nothing but random facts and then later memes when Mary woke up.

We'd just given our order, had gotten a refill on our sweet tea and were discussing whether it would be a good idea for Cobie to go home when the crying started.

One second, Mary was asleep, and the next, she was screaming her head off.

Not nice crying, either. It was pained crying, almost as if something had hurt her.

I frowned and pushed her hair off her head. "What's wrong, baby?"

Mary shook her head, tears streaming down her face.

"Is she hot?" Cobie asked, reaching forward to place her hand on Mary's forehead.

I felt, too, but didn't notice that she was fevered.

"No," I hesitated. "Not really."

At this point, a minute after she'd started, I started to really worry.

Mary didn't usually cry. In fact, it was rare for her to even be unhappy. She was literally the most even-tempered baby that I'd ever met, which was what concerned me.

Mary only ever cried when she was sick, and she'd had an ear infection twice since Marianne had dropped her into my lap.

Since then, I'd learned to read the signs. Only without a fever, and without her pulling at her ear, I wasn't sure that was it this time.

"Is she teething?" Cobie asked, running her finger along Mary's jaw.

"Keep that fucked up kid under control, or get it the fuck out of here. Nobody wants to listen to that nonsense."

Everything inside of me stilled.

My annoyance at Drake, who wouldn't stop looking at Mary like she was a nuisance, vanished. My desire to get up and leave because Mary was throwing an unholy fit—which toddlers did do every now and then, stilled. And my worry for Cobie as she started to look uncomfortable the longer she sat in the hard booth waiting for our food, dissipated.

I stood up, slowly, and hitched Mary up higher against my chest.

"Sir," the young waitress looked at me like she would rather be anywhere else. "We're going to have to ask you to leave. A number of our patrons have expressed difficulty eating their meals because of her screams."

I didn't bother to tell her that I was already planning on leaving.

Instead, I looked over at Cobie.

"Come on," I growled.

Cobie stood, her face showing her discomfort, but she didn't slow in her movements—though they weren't any faster than her norm as of late.

"I'll bag your food up."

The waitress shouldn't have bothered, but before I could tell her that, Cobie patted my arm. "I'll wait in here for it and bring it out with me, okay?"

My jaw clenched, and I nodded my head at the same time that Mary screeched rather loudly into my ear.

I looked over at my girl, saw the tears and unhappiness streaming down her face, and decided that before I said anything I'd regret later, I'd better go.

"Okay," I grunted, then walked to the door.

"Thank fuckin' God," I heard a male voice say. Drake again. "Fuckin' fucked up kid shouldn't be here if she's going to act like that."

Fucking fucked up kid.

Fucking. Fucked up. Kid.

And that's when I lost it.

But, since Mary was still in my arms, now pulling at her ear rather roughly, I kept my feet moving forward even though I wanted to turn around and slam that guy's stupid face into the fucking table he was pounding on.

The old Dante would've let it go. The old Dante who'd been all about not making a scene? Yeah, he was gone. He was buried with my children and wife.

The new Dante?

Well, he didn't give one single fuck about making a scene.

Placing Mary in the car seat and strapping her in, I closed the door very softly, then marched right back inside.

I met Cobie on the way out and handed her the keys. "Start it up, will you?"

Cobie looked at me, looked at the truck, then back at me again.

Then she nodded and walked to the truck, stiffly.

I hesitated, seeing that she was very uncomfortable now, and closed my eyes.

After taking a deep, calming breath, I turned back around, opened the door for Cobie, took the food from her hand and placed it on the floorboard, then snatched the keys from Cobie's hands.

It was when I was rounding the truck's nose that I saw Drake was now standing in the doorway glaring at me.

He didn't say a word as I got into my truck and that's probably what saved him from having his face beat in.

CHAPTER 15

*I may look like a potato now, but one day I'll be
that tasty basket of fries and you'll want me then.*

-Cobie's secret thoughts

Cobie

Day 12 Post Surgery

Was there anything sexier than seeing a man, holding a sick baby who had an ear infection, shirtless?

No. I didn't think there was, either.

I may be under the weather, but my body wasn't dead.

And the things I was feeling for the man that was clearly only ever going to be my friend was quite scary.

Day 13 Post Surgery

I shivered and pulled the quilt off the back of the couch, wrapping it around both Mary—who'd been in my lap for over an hour now just lying there—and myself.

She snuggled down into the quilt, her little fingers touching a patterned heart.

My eyes zeroed in on the heart, and I realized that the quilt wasn't just a quilt.

On the back of the couch, how it had been folded, it looked just like a chevron patterned quilt.

But on the other side was anything but a plain quilt.

Hundreds of squares of tiny little outfits were sewn onto twelve-by-twelve squares.

Some of them were the entire outfit. While other outfits were tilted so you could see the tiny neckline of a onesie or the patterned smiling face embroidered on the foot of a sleeper.

It was darling. And in an instant, I knew that these outfits were the clothes that Dante's kids had worn growing up.

One, in particular, brought my attention to it. A tiny little onesie, the size of a preemie at most, was in the center of the quilt. The front read "Daddy Loves Me" on it.

And my heart broke.

I ran the edge of my finger over it. Saw the yellow stain on one side of the onesie that was either from formula or breast milk. There was no way to really tell without asking.

And I felt a tear leak out of my eye.

God.

My eyes flicked up to Mary, and I wondered if Dante had thought to save any of her clothes.

Marianne wouldn't have had a chance to save any, would she?

It was the first quilt I'd seen like it. Likely not every parent saved all those clothes. But I knew, if the impossible ever happened and I became a parent, I'd save them. Then I'd make something exactly like it.

I'd just repositioned, moving Mary to rest a little more comfortably in the crook of my leg, and tried to ignore the pain.

While I was doing that, Mary chose that moment to throw up.

Whatever green she'd eaten earlier projectiled everywhere. All over the quilt, all over the floor.

And some of it even hit the wall.

Oh, no.

"Dante!"

He came running, and at first, he wasn't mad. Then he saw the quilt, and his entire body strung tight like a bowstring.

He gently pulled Mary up and out of my arms, walking away without a word.

I got up myself, folded the quilt into itself, and took it to the laundry room.

My intention was to clean it, but within moments of me getting to the laundry room with it, he followed me in there, ripped it out of my hands, and walked it out to the garage without another word.

I followed him, watched as he took the quilt to the trash, then angrily slammed it down. The lid followed.

Without a word or a glance at me, he stormed back inside and shut the door.

I went to the trash, pulled the quilt out, and then took it back inside.

He was nowhere to be seen, which worked out.

With what little strength I had, I washed the quilt. Cleaned it, dried it, and then laid it back delicately on the couch.

All the while Dante stayed sequestered in his room.

Day 14 Post Surgery

"Today you need to write your eviction letter," Dante ordered.

I blinked, then turned.

"Have you heard any more?"

Dante nodded.

"Jack got the number off the side of the box. From what I was able to understand, it's ammo. Not the guns that they were originally thinking. The ammo itself is all military surplus, though. It was sold at an auction for pennies on the dollar due to the sheer amount that was sold. However, the buyer was a guy out of Florida. He reported the shipment missing about a month ago. Apparently, this is connected to some case that Rafe is working on, but that's all he would give me. I hadn't even realized he was working a case, so whatever we did helped him out. However, we're all agreed that you should evict him. Rafe, I think, is hoping that they'll move the shipment to where other stolen items are being held—in which I'm not supposed to know about. So, don't go sharing that I know."

He gave me a pointed look, and I saluted him.

"Sir. Yes, sir."

He rolled his eyes at me.

Then flicked the tip of my nose with one blunt finger.

It made my breath catch.

Day 15 Post Surgery

Dante and Mary were in Mary's room. Dante was trying to get Mary asleep, and Mary was fighting it with everything she had. Dante would get her to sleep, though, hopefully for the night.

I was standing in the middle of the kitchen, starving.

So hungry, in fact, that I'd actually been able to get up and find myself something to eat instead of waiting for Dante.

Dante did TV dinners.

He did a lot of sandwiches, and he also did a lot of frozen corn dogs.

What he did not do was cook—at least well. He tried, yes. But trying and excelling were two different things.

Craving something hot that didn't come out of a box that wasn't housing frozen food, I took it upon myself to look through his cabinets.

His mother had come over and stocked the pantry the day before, and my eyes lit on the box of macaroni that was just sitting on the shelf.

Not wanting to bother Dante, I shuffled to the cabinets and started to open them. I didn't stop until I found a pot big enough to fit two boxes of macaroni.

Once I had it going—my chest starting to ache—I'd walked to the fridge to get a drink.

Opening both doors out of habit, my eyes lit on the ice cream.

Smiling, I pulled it out, placed it on the counter, and then shuffle-walked to the cabinet I'd seen the bowls in earlier.

Once I had a bowl and a spoon, I went back to the table and took a seat.

It took me another five minutes before I could find the strength to scoop any ice cream out. Another five to get the lid back on and look at my pitiful amount of ice cream—who knew how many muscles you worked that were in your chest—which also happened to be sore?

So, there I was, sitting there, eating my ice cream and waiting for the water to boil on the stove when Dante came in.

At first, he only smiled when he saw me there.

But then his eyes lit on the bowl—a cute little pink bowl that said 'Yum!' on it.

His eyes went all wonky, and he left the room without another word.

I never saw him again that evening, but in the middle of the night when I got up for a glass of water, I saw the same bowl broken into about ten pieces in the trash. Along with the spoon that I'd used— another one that was shaped differently than all the others.

And that was when I realized that they must've been his wife's, and he most certainly didn't like me using them.

Day 16 Post Surgery

Mary was back. And when I say Mary was back, I meant she was back. There were no more fevers. No more sitting still in anybody's lap, mine or her daddy's. No more throwing up. And there was no more up all night, sleep all day. She was back on her routine. She was back to her grandmother's, and I was back left alone.

Only, I wasn't left alone at my own house. I was left alone at Dante's house.

Dante's house that was covered with another woman's life.

There were signs of his family everywhere.

On the mantle. On the walls. In the bathroom with the pretty pink towels.

So, I wasn't sure what to do.

I didn't want to overstep any boundaries that I couldn't see. Which meant that I literally sat on the couch, or on the bed he'd ordered me to sleep in, and I hadn't ventured anywhere.

Dante left at seven in the morning. He got home at five in the evening. I never once moved but to go to the bathroom.

Hell, I hadn't even eaten.

I was scared to.

My stomach was practically eating itself, and I was on the verge of crying because I was told not to take pain medication on an empty stomach.

I'd already planned on weaning myself off of the good drugs, but I hadn't meant to get off of them *that* early.

Dante walked in the door with a box of chicken hanging off of one finger by the little paper handle, a gallon of sweet tea off of another finger, and Mary's diaper bag hooked on another.

Mary was on his hip, and the moment that they both got inside, I smiled.

It was a tired smile.

One that clearly relayed how much pain I was in, causing Dante to immediately zero his eyes in on me.

"You in pain?"

Couldn't hide anything from him, I supposed.

"A little," I lied.

I was in a whole fuckin' lot of pain.

Hence not bothering to get up and move over the last two hours.

Hell, I'd been stuck watching old reruns of *Roseanne* for the last two hours because the remote had dropped on the floor when I'd sat down after going to the bathroom.

"You need to eat," he growled.

I wanted to eat. But the act of chewing made my chest hurt—at least at this point.

How? Why? I had no fuckin' clue, but it did.

"Okay," I murmured.

He walked away without another word, and I looked over at Mary as she steadily fed a handful of mashed potatoes into her mouth.

"Good?" I asked her.

"Goo!" she agreed.

Or at least I thought she agreed.

"Here."

I looked up to find Dante heading back toward me, a white pain pill in one hand and a cup of sweet tea in the other.

I reached up to take the pill from him, but the act of lifting my arm caused everything to scream at me not to do it.

My hand dropped back to the table.

He looked at me, eyes hard and angry, and brought the pill up to my lips using two fingers.

I opened my mouth, tried to swallow the pill, and nearly choked when it got hung in the back of my throat.

He gave an exasperated sound, brought the cup up to my lips, and tilted it.

I swallowed greedily, then pulled away when I was finished.

"Thank you," I whispered.

Dante's lips twitched. "Welcome."

Day 17 Post Surgery

I took my pain pills today.

I also ordered pizza around lunchtime when I started to get hungry.

And by ordering it, I meant that I texted Hannah—who'd given me her phone number if I ever needed anything—and begged her to bring me something to eat.

She did, but not without asking questions.

"I know that you are hungry, but I remember Dante's mother grocery shopping. She filled her cart nearly all the way up. There's no way you don't have enough food here."

I looked down at my feet.

"A few days ago, I tried to eat ice cream. He saw me eating the ice cream in the bowl and then smashed the bowl to smithereens, I assume it belonged to his wife. A few days before that, I covered up with his quilt made out of his children's baby clothes. Mary threw up on it. He threw it away."

Hannah's eyes looked understanding.

Day 18 Post Surgery

"Oreos shouldn't be anything but the original," he said, staring with dawning horror at the screen, which showed the newest Oreo trend. "That's goddamned disgusting."

I agreed, but I never gave up the chance to play devil's advocate.

My grandfather had taught me that arguing was good. It showed that you had a vested interest in what you were speaking about. That you were passionate. Quick-witted.

God, I missed him.

"They don't look too bad," I said. "And pumpkin spice is the trend in the fall."

He looked at me like I was speaking in tongues. "You're honestly going to tell me that you think Pumpkin Spice Oreos are going to be any good?"

I kept my smile hidden. "I'll let you know when I try them. They have potential."

He gagged. "Gross."

"Let me guess," I drawled. "You probably only like the original ones. The ones that have the normal layer of cream on them."

He raised his brows at me. "Is that a bad thing?"

"More cream is always better," I found myself saying.

I didn't agree with that. In fact, I loved the thin ones. The ones that had a very minimal layer of cream. My favorite part was the cookie itself.

"Whatever you say."

I grinned as I turned my eyes back to the television screen. But the grin wasn't due to my argument that I'd started. It was due to the fact that he'd smiled.

Smiled.

And it damn near stopped my heart.

"I like it when you smile," I found myself saying.

Dante's smile slowly fell from his face, but his eyes stayed on mine.

"Haven't really had a reason to smile lately," he murmured. "I haven't laughed like I have the last two weeks since…*they* died."

His inability to say the actual words—since my wife and children died—was telling.

I looked over at where Mary was asleep on the couch.

"You have her," I murmured. "And you now have me. Don't let it go so long again."

Dante winked.

He freakin' winked!

And then he turned his eyes back to the TV.

"Yes, ma'am."

Day 19 Post Surgery

I was back in my own home, and that was largely due to the fact that Dante wasn't there to stop me.

I knew I'd hear about it when he got home from work, but it was time.

I was becoming too dependent on him. That, and I was afraid that I was falling in love with him.

In love with a man that I knew was about as emotionally distant as a vacuum cleaner.

So yes, I'd gone home. And yes, I'd decided not to tell him that I was doing it.

Why? Because I knew if I had told him, then he'd have tried his level best to get me to stay.

CHAPTER 16

If you keep pronouncing the L in salmon, I'm going to stab you in the dick with a kah-nife.

-Dante to his brother, Travis

Dante

I arrived home to find it empty. Not just empty of life, but empty of emotion.

Not seeing her in my home was like a blow straight to the sternum.

I tried not to let it bother me that she wasn't there. I also tried not to think about the fact that she didn't tell me she was going. Instead, she'd waited until I was gone, and had snuck out like a thief in the night.

Not a thief.

Just a woman that I was beginning to depend on.

Goddammit.

The worst thing, though?

It was the way Mary walked through the lower level of the house and called out for 'Obie.'

"Mary, girl," I called to my daughter. "You hungry?"

"Obie?"

I walked toward where she was standing next to the couch, her hand on the arm as she patted it.

Yes, that was exactly where Cobie normally was when we got home.

I had a feeling that I'd made her feel somewhat unwelcome since she never seemed to move from the one spot.

The two times that she'd done it, first venturing into the kitchen and eating out of my wife's bowl, and the second time venturing into the laundry room to clean the quilt…well, those two times hadn't been very good for me. I'd literally overreacted, and I'd immediately felt like shit afterward.

I'd thought that we were getting over the timidity, though.

Unfortunately, we hadn't quite overcome that obstacle seeing as she was no longer there.

She'd rather leave without a word than tell me to my face that she was leaving.

Which I couldn't blame her for.

I hadn't been the nicest person in the world to deal with.

"Cobie went home, baby," I said to her as I held my hands out. "You want some dinner?"

"Nuts."

I rolled my eyes. That was Cobie's doing.

Over the course of the last month, Cobie had introduced Mary to quite a few things, peanuts being one of them.

After expressing that peanuts were her favorite snack, I'd gone by the store and gotten her some in a 'party container.'

It was massive and likely had enough nuts in it to last a normal person an entire year. Mary and Cobie, though? Yeah, it lasted them a week.

And now that was all that Mary ever wanted.

Nuts.

Morning, noon, and night.

"You can have a handful, but you're not having that for dinner," I told her, walking into the kitchen with her in my arms. "How does chicken sound?"

I asked this as I opened up the freezer, pulling out a bag of frozen chicken nuggets.

The thought of eating them nearly made my stomach turn, but without Cobie here to eat, there was no reason to open up one of the bigger boxed dinners. I couldn't eat it all myself.

And Cobie didn't eat enough to feed a baby bird.

"Yuck!"

Snorting as I closed the fridge, I turned around and was about to switch the oven on when I heard a knock at the door.

I hesitated with my finger over the 'cook' button and decided to turn it on in a minute.

My irrational heart was hoping that Cobie had come to her senses and returned.

I couldn't have been further from the truth.

After putting Mary down on the ground to play, I walked to the door with a weird sense of hopefulness making my steps hurried.

I opened my door, surprised yet unsurprised to find Ruthie, my wife's—dead wife's—best friend, standing on my doorstep.

Word had gotten out that I'd been at the office. I knew it was only a matter of time until she showed. But I supposed I hadn't expected her to come over so soon.

I'd figured she'd give me more time to get settled, though.

Behind her was her husband, Sterling.

Sterling was a professional baseball player and looked to be sporting a beard that was likely due to playoffs being around the corner.

"Hey, man." I offered my hand. "What are y'all doing here?"

Sterling took it and dropped it. The moment he did, Ruthie threw herself at me.

"I'm so mad at you right now."

I hugged Ruthie, and something welled in my throat.

"I'm sorry."

"I know." She breathed out shakily. "I am, too. I've missed you like crazy."

I didn't know what to say to that.

I wasn't ready to see her.

Wasn't ready to do *anything* or see *anyone* that had to do with my wife. Not clean out her closet. Not call her best friend to make sure she was okay. Hell, I didn't even stop paying the car insurance.

Why?

Because doing any of those things was admitting that she was gone, and I just wasn't there yet.

"Come on in," I ordered, opening the door.

Mary teetered up, her eyes wide and happy, as she welcomed the newcomers into her domain.

"Oh, D," she breathed. "She's beautiful."

I looked at Mary, who'd started to follow me to the door but had been distracted by a butterfly—a fake one that Cobie had given her—on the couch.

"Yeah," I murmured. "She's pretty stinkin' cute."

Sterling grunted. "Got your hair."

She did.

All of my kids always did.

Seemed the blond hair and blue eyes were dominant in my bloodline.

"She does," I confirmed. "And my stubbornness. Mary, come here, girl, and meet Ruthie."

Mary looked at Ruthie, grinned, but turned back to her butterfly.

"What's she got?"

"A friend, Cobie, bought it for her," I murmured. "At the grocery store. It's one of those pencil toppers, but no way in hell was I giving her a pencil to stick it on top of. So, it's just a toy for now."

Before Ruthie could reply to that comment, though, my phone rang.

"Give me a second?" I asked.

Ruthie waved me away and went to Mary. Sterling, on the other hand, didn't move.

He stayed exactly where he was and waited for me to take the call. Which I did.

"Rafe."

"You better be glad that we put eyes on him, and then had his ass kicked out of that place."

"Why?"

Now I was curious. Though, anything that had to do with Drake made me curious.

I didn't like the guy, and never had.

My brother, Reed, had always been best friends with the stupid joke of a human being. But Drake never showed his true colors in front of Reed—at least not totally. He only showed them behind Reed's back, and I fucking hated the douche more than life when he was hanging around.

Now, well, now it'd only gotten worse.

"Because Drake started to burn her motherfuckin' house down. My guess is that he has insurance on it—renter's insurance. He'd get a good chunk of change from it. That, and he stole whatever he was storing. Loaded it up with the tractor that likely belongs to Cobie, straight into a U-Haul. Shit's at a warehouse. I'm thinking about giving an anonymous tip that there are drugs in it. They'll bring out a K-9, and his ass'll get busted."

I knew he wouldn't do that. Not when he wanted to know where the other stolen merchandise was.

But I did see him sharing an anonymous tip with the person Drake was 'storing' the belongings for, just to see what they'd do.

"Is he out now, though?"

I'd helped Cobie construct an excuse for her having to kick the poor bastard out of her house. I'd even gone to drop off the certified letter that would ensure he did, in fact, know about the upcoming eviction.

According to the post office, it'd been delivered two days later.

"Yep," he confirmed. "Though, when the cops showed, he said he was burning trash. We couldn't share stuff on our end without tipping our hand to the poor sod, though. So we chose to let it lie.

Hopefully by doing so we didn't shoot ourselves in the foot. We really need Drake to be found by his renters. That can't happen with him in jail."

No, it couldn't.

"Anything you want me to do?"

"Nope," Rafe instantly replied. "You just stay your ass where you're at. I don't want you to run your mouth and fuck my chances of finding out what's happening related to my other case."

I rolled my eyes. "Do you actually work at all?"

Rafe chuckled. "When I feel like it."

I shook my head. "I saw you didn't get paid but for fifteen hours last week. At least you're not swindling me."

Rafe laughed as he hung up.

"Problems?"

"Kind of," I muttered. "But I was told they're not my problems, so I'm to stay out of it."

Sterling grunted, sounding lazy, but I knew he'd taken in everything.

Sterling used to be a Navy SEAL, and you never stopped being a Navy SEAL. He may be a professional baseball player now, but that didn't mean that his mind wasn't as sharp as it'd been a few years ago when he'd been on the SEAL Team.

"You need anything, let me know, okay?"

"I'm not a slouch, Ling-Ling."

Sterling flipped me off at my use of the name his kids called him.

I winked and pushed the phone back into my pocket, but as my eyes caught on the blanket that I'd covered Cobie up with just last night, I realized two things.

One, I wasn't okay with Cobie leaving the way she did.

Two, I needed to talk to Ruthie, and I needed her to give me her honest advice.

***

An hour later, Ruthie and I sat on my front porch while Sterling watched TV on the couch with my daughter. He'd done it on purpose, of course, giving Ruthie and I time to discuss what she'd come here to discuss.

"It's been years, D."

I knew that.

I felt every single one of those years in my heart.

"Yeah," I croaked. "It has."

"And it's been enough time that you're allowed to move on," she continued.

I knew that, too.

"It's time to stop hiding."

I didn't feel like I was hiding.

"I'm not hiding," I told her. "I'm trying to recover."

"You're hiding."

"I'm not…"

"Why did it take you this long to come back here?"

I didn't have anything to say to that.

I couldn't stand to be here without my family in it.

The only reason I was back now was because of Mary.

"Why are all those doors up there locked?" she asked. "Why aren't you sleeping in your bed?"

"How do you…"

"I saw the spare bed in Mary's room. I'm not dumb, and don't act like I am."

That was right. Ruthie had gone up earlier to change Mary's diaper, and she must've seen it then.

Shit.

"Ruthie…"

"Lily wouldn't want you to live like this."

I opened my mouth to retort her statement when she continued.

"Lily told me once, when I got out of prison, that she would never want somebody to live such a lonely existence as I'd once been living."

Ruthie had killed her husband. Ruthie also had a valid reason—her husband, once my best friend, had beat her so ruthlessly that he'd made her miscarry. She protected herself, but in the process, had killed her husband.

She was convicted of murder, but only served a few years as opposed to her original multiple year sentence.

Silas, Ruthie's cell mate's husband, had gone to pick her up the day she was released, and I remembered the very conversation Ruthie was speaking of.

"Lily loved you with all her heart," I found myself saying. "And you're right. She would've never wanted anyone to live the existence you were subjecting yourself to. But, things are different… my life… Lily was the one, Ruthie."

She stared at me for so long that a lesser man would've started to squirm. She saw things differently, and always had.

"If the situations were reversed, would you want Lily to be happy?"

I blinked.

"The selfish part of me would want her to never have anyone else," I told her honestly.

"But…"

"But, the other part, the part that was happy that Lily was happy, would've wanted her to find something after I was gone."

"And why don't you deserve the same?"

I didn't have anything to say to that.

"I'm trying, Ruthie."

"You're not trying," she countered. "You're using every excuse you can find not to move on. You have Mary, and she pulled you out of the darkness, but you have to do the rest. You have to want to live, and you can't do that while you still cling to your dead wife. She doesn't want you to live like this. Nobody wants you to live like this."

I gritted my teeth.

"Ruthie…"

"It's time."

It wasn't time. It'd never be time.

Would it?

***

"If I died, how long would you wait to move on?"

I looked over at my wife.

"At least six months. Maybe three if the girl was hot," I teased.

Lily punched my arm and then burst out laughing.

"Seriously, though. If I died tomorrow, would you move on, or wallow in a vat of self-pity?" She looked at me, all seriousness in her eyes.

I shrugged. "I would move on. I would find a way to live because of the kids. Why?"

"I read a book today," she said, shrugging. "It was a time travel romance. She traveled to his time, they fell in love, and then she was transported back. She meets his reincarnated self on the plane that she was transported back to, and they knew instantly who the other was. He, on the other hand, had to live the rest of his life by himself. He died with no kids. No nothing. Meanwhile, she's pregnant, and meets his ghost seconds after she returns."

Lily read. A lot. This book, though, sounded like dog shit.

"That book sounds like it sucks," I told her.

She rolled her eyes. "I thought it was beautiful, but it made me sad for him. Why was he the one that had to make all the sacrifices? Would she have been mad had he moved on? She was actually happy, when she got back and read his 'history,' that he hadn't had a wife or kids. Happy. I, on the other hand, thought that was kind of selfish."

I pulled my wife into my side and closed my eyes.

Lily always started conversations when we were in bed. Always, right before I was seconds away from falling asleep for the night.

But for her, I'd stay awake. I loved her.

I loved her with all of my heart, and always would.

"I think every situation is different," I told her honestly, my eyes heavy with sleep. "Say, for instance, you decided to up and croak on me. I would move on only in the sense that I'd put one foot in front of the other. I'd do just about anything for the kids. But moving on to another woman wouldn't be one of them."

"I would want you to move on," she whispered.

"You can want in one hand, and shit in the other, and see which one fills up faster."

She squealed in outrage and shoved a tiny fist straight into my ribs.

"Ouch," I laughed, rolling over until she was pinned underneath me. "Wench."

She giggled, then sobered. "Dante."

"Yeah, baby?"

"Don't live a life you think will honor my memory. If you ever found somebody, I'd want you to be happy. Just like I know you'd want me to be happy if that ever happened."

"It'll never happen. So this is a moot point, anyway."

***

I woke struggling to breathe as I recalled the memory that played through my dreams.

"It'll never happen. So this is a moot point, anyway."

Except it had happened.

It'd happened, and I was so pissed at Lily for it happening.

So fucking pissed that she wasn't here anymore.

But one thing she said held true. I would've wanted her to be happy.

And she had wanted me to be, also.

Could I take that step in Cobie's direction?

I wasn't really sure.

I wasn't sure about damn near everything nowadays.

One thing I was sure about, though, and that was that I missed Cobie.

Didn't I owe it to myself—and Lily—to find out why I missed her?

CHAPTER 17

How soon into a friendship can you start calling them a motherfucker?

-Asking for a friend

Cobie

One week later

I'd never, not ever, wanted to do anything more than I wanted to call Dante.

I wanted to hear his voice. I wanted to see his little girl hug her arms around his neck. I wanted to freakin' have a conversation with him that was about stupid shit like what the weatherman was wearing.

What I didn't want to do was admit that I'd gone and fallen in love with the man. Why? Because the man wasn't ever going to fall in love with me back. His heart was already promised to another, and that would just be plain dumb for me to go and do.

So, I suppressed the twitch to reach for the phone and went about my day.

It'd been a total of four weeks since I'd had my surgery, and I was starting to feel like myself again—at least myself minus boobs.

It was still weird to put on a T-shirt and not have that added feeling of wearing a bra underneath. Things rubbed weird, and I even contemplated wearing a sports bra just because the feeling was so odd.

Yet, I ignored the new and untried feelings, or at least tried to, anyway.

Hell, even the chest part of my seatbelt fit wrong.

Before, it used to go between my breasts.

Now, it went somewhere to the right, rubbing all sorts of different places.

Then there was the way I used to sleep—which was on my side. Now it felt uncomfortable because I couldn't find that used-to-be favorite position anymore. With my boobs missing, I tended to lay more toward my belly rather than on my side.

It was week four, day twenty-six, and I had nothing to do.

Tomorrow was my week four appointment with the doctor, and tomorrow they might tell me I could go back to work.

Likely, though, he'd tell me to take the full six weeks that he'd told me was normal, and I'd have to tell him that if I stayed one more extra day at home, I might very well die.

My job was the only thing keeping me sane at this point, the thought of being there, instead of in this house all alone, sounded so appealing it wasn't even funny.

Dante freakin' haunted me.

His laughter echoed inside my brain. Though, he didn't laugh all that much. Once that I knew of for sure, and it'd been because of something Mary had done to me.

But it was enough to remind me of everything that I was missing. That he was missing.

I felt like he was cheating himself, holding himself aloft of all things that might make him happy. Even when he was there, he wasn't really 'there.'

I was so engrossed in my thoughts of Dante that I hadn't been paying attention to what was in front of me. I.e., the steps of my porch before I was nearly falling down them.

And what caught me weren't my own arms, but the arms of a man that was the star of my every waking and sleeping moments.

"Dante," I breathed, pain from my sudden movements arcing through my belly and chest. "Wh-what are you doing here?"

Dante scowled. "You left."

I blinked. "I left a week ago. Did it take you a week to notice?"

He scowled harder. "No. What took me a week to do was find out where you were."

I blinked again. "I've always been here."

"You weren't here. I came by every single day, at different times of the day."

"I went for a walk every single day… and yesterday I walked and went to the grocery store. It's just sometimes I don't have the energy to do it until later in the day. While some days I wake up and can go right then because I have the want and desire."

He sighed.

"You haven't been avoiding me?"

I shook my head. "Never."

I would never, not ever, avoid this man.

That was part of my problem, and also why I'd left. I didn't want to follow him around like a puppy like I had been doing.

He set me up on my feet and then let me go, but his hands lingered at my waist for a few long moments as he waited to see if I had my footing.

"You want to go get something to eat with me?"

I didn't even think to decline.

"Absolutely!"

***

"I don't like this."

I looked up to find Dante staring at the couple across the diner from us. And when I say across, I mean just a table's length away. It was a small diner. One that was quaint, small, and tucked into the backwoods of Uncertain, Texas. The lake was less than a hundred yards away, and the water looked like glass.

The trees were just on the verge of losing their leaves, and the Spanish moss hanging from the trees was just starting to turn white.

"What don't you like?" the man asked the girl.

"I don't like that it told everyone that I was driving. Who does Apple think they are, telling me whether I can or can't text and drive?"

Dante stiffened across from me.

"Just turn it off. I heard it's in settings or something," the man said distractedly, his eyes scanning the menu.

"I shouldn't have to. I should be able to text anyone I want to text. It's my phone, not theirs. If I want to put my life in danger—which I'm not because I know where all the freakin' letters are—I should be able to do that."

My brows rose at that statement. Dante's, though? They lowered. Then he surprised the hell out of me by looking down at his water glass and clenching his jaw. His hands clutched the edge of the table, and the muscles in his arms bunched. Like he was struggling. Like he was trying to keep himself seated the only way he knew how. Brute force.

"Do what you want."

"Texting isn't even that bad. I mean, I don't even have to look at the screen when I do it."

The man with her snorted.

Dante lost it.

He stood up, pulled his phone out of his pocket, did something on the screen, and then placed it nicely on the table in front of the woman.

"That's my wife and two kids," he said softly. "They're dead now because a teenage girl thought it would be okay to answer a text. It wasn't okay. My sister didn't react well. They went over a bridge and drowned. My wife was knocked unconscious after the impact with the river. My daughters both drowned, and I listened to them through the phone that my wife was using to talk to me on. So, you may not think it's necessary to use that app. And that's your prerogative. However, maybe stop and think about somebody other than yourself."

With that, Dante walked back over to our table, gave me a look that said to follow him, and left without another word.

I watched him walk all the way out. I stopped, looked over at the table next to me, and sighed.

Standing up, I looked longingly at the food I was about to order and followed him out the door seconds later.

Dante was sitting on his motorcycle that was parked next to my car.

"You still want to go?"

He nodded once.

"You up for a ride?"

I took stock of my body.

I was still residually sore. The doctor said it could take up to three months for the pain and weakness to go away completely.

"It's like losing a limb. That doesn't go away overnight."

But I felt pretty good. Really, I did.

That's why I nodded my head and said, "I'd love to."

But once I got up to his side where he was straddling his bike, I didn't know what to do from there.

And I covered my nervousness by chattering his ear off.

"I've never been on a motorcycle before. In fact, I've always wanted to ride one, but I've never known anyone that had one to ask them."

Dante grunted, keeping his eyes forward, and I bit my lip and wondered if this was a good idea—placing my body up against his back.

I didn't know how he'd react. I didn't know if he'd be okay with me touching him after what had happened in there.

But the moment I placed my hands on his shoulder and swung my leg over, he seemed to relax.

The moment I placed my hands on his hips, he started to chuckle.

"Gonna need to get closer than that," he murmured, circling his fingers around my wrists and tugging lightly on them.

I scooted forward until I was pressed to him, crotch to chest, and waited for what he'd do next.

He started the bike.

Shocker.

What was a shocker, though, was the fact that he took my hands and encircled them around his chest.

Once I had a hold of his shirt—because my arms couldn't fit all the way around his broad chest—he let go.

I didn't.

Not until we finished our ride, and wound up at some house off Caddo Lake.

Apparently, there was a motorcycle club—MC—that he knew there. They were having a party, and he'd been invited multiple times. He'd turned them down so much that he almost felt compelled to go to one. He didn't tell me why he'd never gone, but I knew as soon as I arrived why he never went.

There were a lot of happy couples in attendance.

It was hard to see other people happy when you weren't happy yourself. I knew that from experience.

But, for once, I didn't feel so alone with Dante standing at my side.

Not when the club president, a man named Peek at our sides and expressed his happiness in seeing us there. Dante more than me.

Something passed between the two men as we grabbed ourselves a plate of food that was cold, but still good.

And I wouldn't know until much later on in the night as we were saying goodbye to the MC, that Dante, according to quite a few women that introduced themselves, actually looked quite happy.

And that was because of me.

I didn't believe them.

Not at all.

CHAPTER 18

You're not done licking until she pushes you off.

-Words of wisdom

Cobie

"Stupid. So stupid."

I groaned inwardly as I tried to remember why it would be a bad idea to call Dante, or maybe even text him, and ask him what he was doing.

I shouldn't care about what he is doing! Really, I shouldn't!

But I did.

I really, really cared.

So much, in fact, that when I was in the grocery store, I almost sent him a picture of the new Oreos. This time they were peanut butter and jelly flavored.

Very gross sounding. But did that stop me from buying the damn things?

No.

In fact, I bought two!

I was so distracted as I sat in my car, the package of Oreos in my lap, that I wasn't paying attention to the man that pulled up next to the bridge until he'd already blocked my way out of the parking lot.

I watched from my spot as a man got out of the truck, walked over to the side of the bridge, and tossed the bag down.

I didn't know what made me not go another way, nor did I know why I watched instead of sending that text. I couldn't really tell you what pull that was practically urging me to go, but I went.

The minute he pulled away, I pulled up where his truck had previously been parked.

The moment it was in park, I got out, locked the door, and hurried down the steep embankment that led to the river below.

My eyes scanned the area, looking for the blue bag, and I winced when I saw it floating in the river about ten yards downstream from where I was standing, and about four yards out from the bank.

I'd have to get wet to go get that bag.

But the inexplicable pull was there, urging me forward despite my fear of the water.

I didn't know why I had a fear of water. It wasn't like I'd had a trauma related to water, but I'd never really liked it.

Not ever.

But I didn't let it stop me from walking down the bank. And eventually wading into the water.

I was just glad I could see down to the bottom. I don't think I could've been able to wade in without seeing what I was doing.

Wading in up to my thighs—thank God I'd worn shorts today—I reached for the blue canvas bag and drug it toward me.

And that's when I saw that the bag was moving.

Motherfucking moving.

I pulled it with me to the bank, then walked a few more yards before setting the bag down.

There, I crouched and unzipped the bag.

At first, I wasn't sure what it was. The inside of the bag was wet, saturating the animal that lay inside.

At first, I thought it was a ferret because of its long gray body, but then I saw the paws, and instantly realized it was a cat.

Then I saw the kitty's face and realized rather quickly that something was wrong with the poor little creature.

He didn't look like he had a nose. The holes were there, but the ridge and tilt that usually signaled a cat's nose were missing. His eyes were a little too far apart, and I didn't know if it was due to his lack of nose, or if they actually were far apart.

Whatever he was, the poor thing was soaked, scared, and shivering.

"You poor little thing," I cooed, pulling him out and placing his wet body against my chest.

The kitten gave a pitiful mewl and burrowed closer.

An hour later, I texted a picture of the little guy to Dante, instantly getting a response.

Dante (11:33 am): what made you go get the bag??

Me (11:34 am): It might've been due to the particular bag that he'd tossed in that gave it away.

Hell, it also might've been due to the face that he'd tossed it by getting out instead of straight out the window—which I knew he could've accomplished. I didn't know. I was just glad he didn't drown. I felt so bad. *He's still shaking. But look at his fur! It's curly.*

Dante (11:35 am): it's cute. Mary says "mine." Lol.

I grinned but placed the cat in a box in my passenger seat.

After stopping at the dollar store for kitten food and a litter box, I drove home.

Once I had him settled and sitting comfortably in my lap, I then started my paperwork that my job needed for me to start work in another week.

Six weeks was perfectly sufficient after having surgery…wasn't it?

***

Paperwork done, and my new little kitty with a full belly lazing in the sunshine of my porch, I started to clean up the weeds in my flowerbeds.

I was so immersed in what I was doing that I didn't hear the truck pull up at my curb and shut off.

Then again, that was fairly normal. I lived on a somewhat busy street, and cars came up and down this road all day long, twenty-four seven.

Just down the road was a bar, and there were times that I heard music blaring until all hours of the morning.

But that didn't bother me much. I knew when I moved here that it was always like that. It had been when I was growing up, too.

That was one of the things about living downtown in the historical district. The nightlife was always around, celebrating something or other.

I ripped another weed out just as I heard someone's voice behind me.

"You have a cat."

I looked over to see Drake standing on the path that led up to my house. I'd been airing out the place since I hadn't been there in over two weeks. Old places like mine—my grandfather's—had a way of doing that, though.

If old places like mine weren't lived in, then they started to smell musty. At least that's the way I felt.

The cat had drifted out, drawn to the sunshine, and I'd allowed it. He wasn't hurting anything.

I stiffened and turned to find Drake there, his hands in his pockets.

"Yeah."

"It's fucking ugly."

I don't know what made me so mad about hearing those words, but after hearing similar words in regard to him speaking about Mary, I was suddenly very mad.

"I think he's adorable," I snapped.

Drake's eyebrows rose. "You're mad."

I crossed my arms. "What are you doing here?"

"I'm here because you kicked me out of my house."

I had.

While at Dante's, I'd sent a certified letter to Drake saying he had exactly a month to move out of the house because I was putting it up for sale.

I hadn't thought to check to see if he'd actually moved, though. Rafe and Dante had said they'd handle it, and I'd allowed it because I didn't want to have anything to do with the mess that they'd created.

"I'm selling it to help pay for my bills," I said. "I'm sorry. I didn't have any choice. You were the one to point out that I should fight the cancer, weren't you?"

Not altogether a lie. I did have medical bills rolling in, and the sale of my old house would mean that I wouldn't have to live in debt for the next year as I worked to pay them off.

Then again, had I not known that Drake was doing something illegal at my place, I wouldn't have kicked him out. I would've suffered in silence due to him being my best friend's widower.

But he *had* been doing something bad, and though Dante had kept it on the down low, I knew that they'd found something substantial enough to warrant me kicking him out within a few days of finding out that he'd been doing something that I might not agree with.

"I think that's a bullshit answer," he countered. "Marianne told me you had a lot of money, thanks to your grandfather dying. This house would sell for upwards of a mil. You didn't have to sell the one I was living in."

"So, you wanted me to sell the one I was living in?" I countered right back.

His eyes narrowed. "A single woman doesn't need a house like this. One that takes a lot of upkeep. A single woman needs a one-bedroom apartment with security so she doesn't fear for her life."

I shivered slightly as I took in his words.

He was staring at me like I was a nuisance. Like he was pissed off that I'd decided to go forward with the treatment.

Fucker.

"I love this house. This was the place that I grew up. The only place in the world that holds good memories for me. I'm not selling the house I'm living in, regardless of whether you want me to or not. You're not my husband. You're not even my friend.

You're my dead best friend's husband. I'm sorry you were displaced, but I gave you sufficient time to move out and find another place. I'm sorry if you didn't utilize that time wisely. I gave you what was required by law and then some."

Drake narrowed his eyes. "You're not my friend?"

"Drake, I don't even know you. The only time I ever saw you was with Marianne, and even then, it was sparingly. To be honest, I felt like you hated me. You saw I was around, and immediately left the room. I think the most time we spent with each other was right after Marianne's death, but that was only because I was helping you with funeral arrangements."

The only contact we had was when I got the check from him each month for rent. We'd share a few words, maybe a short conversation, but that was it. There was nothing more to Drake and me.

"Why were you with Dante?"

I frowned.

"Why not?"

"I don't like him."

I didn't know what to say to that.

"He and Marianne shared a fling. They have a baby together. A baby they conceived while we were still very much married. When she got sick, she came home, but that was only because she knew that I could afford the chemo treatments and he couldn't." He narrowed his eyes. "And now you're with him. You were supposed to be my friend."

"I met Dante six weeks ago. He helped me when I needed it most. He was a friend when I didn't think I needed one. He's a good man, and I don't know what happened with Marianne and him. I've tried valiantly not to think about it. Yes, they do share a kid."

He knew that, right? "But from what I understand, it was Marianne that deceived him, and not the other way around. Dante never knew that Marianne was married, or he wouldn't have done a single thing with her. I guarantee that."

And I did.

I knew with all my heart and soul that Dante wouldn't have slept with Marianne had he known the full details of what had taken place. He would've stayed far, far away from her.

Yet, he hadn't.

Which led me to believe that Marianne hadn't shared a single detail about her relationship with Drake.

Hell, I wasn't even sure she shared anything about herself even after he knew Marianne was married.

"Dante's not a good guy."

My brows rose.

"You don't believe me?" he asked. "He's not. I don't think he should have custody of that *kid*."

That kid being Dante's child, Mary, whom he shared with Marianne.

"Why?" I asked.

I was truly curious now.

I'd seen Dante with Mary.

I knew damn well that he was a good father.

"He hurt people."

I wanted to laugh at that pathetic excuse.

"Why?"

"I heard things about what he did to the people that tried to hurt his family. He made his own sister kill herself."

I narrowed my eyes. "He most certainly did not."

"He most certainly did. Did you know that his sister was the one who was driving the car that day that his family died?"

"Yes."

"Did you know that she was on drugs?"

I clenched my jaw.

"He knew that she was a few days later. I was in town that day that he confronted her in the hospital. I was there with Marianne."

I didn't show my feelings at all.

I kept my eyes straight forward and refused to say anything.

"He yelled at her and made her cry. It's just convenient that she killed herself, right?"

I didn't know what to say to that.

"My sister killed herself because she was raped for years by a boy who came over every weekend to spend time with my brother," Dante said. "She was upset that she'd killed my family, but I, in no way, shape or form, yelled at her because of that. I was too lost in my own goddamn grief to ever say anything to her. It took me six months to finally talk to my family. I was yelling at the hospital because they wouldn't let me see my children. I needed confirmation that they were actually gone."

I turned to find Dante standing in my front entryway, staring daggers at Drake.

"What are you doing in her house?" Drake snarled. "Get out!"

Dante didn't bother to move.

"This is unforgivable, she's mine."

My brows rose at that, and at first, I thought he was talking about Mary. Until I felt Dante's hand circle my hip.

"She's mine," he countered. "Whether you like it or not."

I didn't know what in the hell was going on, but I could tell whatever it was, Drake didn't like it. Not at all.

"Wrong move, D."

"Right move, Drake."

I blinked, looked up at Dante in question, and heard the angry growl come from the man in front of me.

Dante dropped his eyes to mine and then turned to watch Drake—who was stalking angrily down the length of my walkway.

He got into his truck, slammed the door closed, and then roared off before I could think of saying goodbye.

Not that I would've said goodbye.

But still.

I waited until Drake was farther down the road before turning to Dante. "When did you get here?"

I hadn't heard him pull up, either.

Dante's lips twitched.

"Mary wanted to see the kitty."

I grinned and turned in his arms to see Mary on the porch petting my new friend.

I shrugged Dante's arm away and crouched next to Mary, who had my new kitty by the torso and was burying her face into his neck.

"You like my kitty, Mary?" I questioned my favorite girl.

Mary looked up and smiled. "Yes!"

Mary knew a few words, two of those she pronounced really well. 'Yes' and 'no.'

I giggled and ran my hand over Mary's blonde ringlets.

"What should we name him?"

Mary closed her pretty blue eyes and then opened them again.

"Cacker."

"Cracker?"

Then she shook her head. "Wacker?"

I bit my lip. "Ummm…"

"Yes!"

"Yes, what?"

"Yum!"

I started to laugh. "You want to name him Yum?"

"Yum-Yum." She nodded her head in confirmation.

I snorted and turned to look up at Dante, who was staring down at his child and me with a bemused smile on his face. "Probably shouldn't have asked her."

"I like Yum-Yum," I said. "Yum-Yum it is, right, Mary?"

That's when I got a load of Mary's shirt.

My brows furrowed.

"Ummm, what is she wearing?"

Dante grinned and bent down as he pulled the shirt away from Mary's chest so I could get the full view of the shirt.

"Travis's son, TJ, used to wear this shirt. But it got too small for him, and Mary just had to have it. I couldn't convince her to put on something else, so we're wearing it."

I started to laugh, my eyes skimming over the shirt one more time.

If you think I'm cute now, just wait until my beard comes in.

"Ahhh," I laughed, wiping tears from my eyes.

Dante's smile was heart stopping.

That night, things for us changed.

Became charged.

No longer was it just us being friends. That night, what we had turned into more, and neither of us realized it until it was too late.

CHAPTER 19

Maybe eating a donut wasn't cheating on my diet. Maybe going on a diet was cheating on my donuts.

-Rationale of a hungry person

Cobie

That night Mary fell asleep on the couch at Dante's house with my cat tucked in close to her chest.

We were now at Dante's house due to a water pipe that had burst at the wrecker office about thirty minutes into his visit to see the new kitty.

I'd just gone to the fridge and emerged with a beer for both Dante and me when he scooted over and patted the loveseat beside him so I wouldn't disturb Mary.

We were both on our second beers.

I was downright feeling good, while Dante seemed content... Maybe, dare I say, even happy.

He was all smiles today, despite a pipe bursting in his office and flooding not just his office, but Travis's as well.

After having an emergency water damage clean up company who specialized in this kind of disaster come out and take a look at it, it was determined that it would take over fifteen grand to fix it. Yet Dante only shook his head and laughed, completely bemused by the situation.

Travis had narrowed his eyes at him at the time, but still, Dante's mood hadn't waned.

It was exhilarating to see him smiling despite the shitty things happening around him—like listening to Drake run his mouth when he had no clue what he was talking about and his office being trashed.

Once Dante was sufficiently sequestered to his half of the loveseat, I sat, our thighs only inches apart, and handed him his beer, and immediately felt Dante's warmth.

It had never felt so intimate when I sat this close to him before, and my heart was pounding about a million miles an hour.

We stayed like that, for hours, as we watched rerun after rerun of *How I Met Your Mother.*

We were on our third and fifth beer when I finally fell asleep.

My eyes closed, and I dreamed.

But my dreams weren't sweet like I'd been expecting. They were sad and downright depressing.

***

The dream I was having sucked. It sucked so bad that I couldn't even begin to explain its suckiness. Dante was staring at me, laughing, because I'd told him my feelings for him.

"You really think I could fall for someone like you?"

Everyone else was laughing, too.

"Cobie."

I woke with a start and stared straight into Dante's concerned eyes.

"You okay?"

I blinked, then nodded my head as I raised one hand up and pushed the hair out of my face. "Yeah," I croaked. "I'm fine. What's going on?"

"We fell asleep on the couch," he said. "Your cat is annoying."

My brows rose, but with it being so dark, I couldn't figure out why, exactly, he thought my cat was annoying.

"He's been digging his claws into my beard for over an hour. Can you make him go away? I can't seem to lift my hands."

I laughed and reached up and over, half of my body draping over Dante's, as I picked the cat up and pulled him to my chest to cuddle.

I didn't, however, move off of Dante.

I kept my body exactly where it was, and tried to forget the dream that he'd woken me from.

"Not really a dream, though. More of a nightmare."

"What?" I asked, startled.

"Your dream. You said, 'It was just a dream,' when you woke up. But I wouldn't call something that made you cry out like that in your sleep a dream. I'd classify it as a nightmare. You sounded like you were in pain."

I was.

"Oh," I murmured, eyes once again closing. "I can't even seem to remember it now."

I snuggled in closer to Dante, who didn't push me away, and was asleep again moments later.

Not once did I notice that we weren't on the couch anymore. Nor did I notice that I'd somehow lost my pants, and Dante's chest was smooth underneath my fingers.

Because if I had, maybe I wouldn't have stayed.

If I had, maybe what happened next wouldn't have happened.

CHAPTER 20

*If your woman isn't the most annoying person on
the planet, she's not the woman for you.*

-Cobie to Dante

Cobie

This dream was way better, was my first conscious thought.

I pushed back against the hard column of Dante's cock that I could feel along my backside and groaned.

"Dante," I breathed.

His big hand went to my hip and he pulled me back as he ground himself against me, not saying a word.

I didn't need words, though. Not when it came to the man that had stolen my heart.

Dante wasn't much of a talker. It didn't surprise me that that extended to sex.

He growled, though, and that was just as good, if not better.

"Please." I pushed back against him.

His hand smoothed up under my shirt to lay flat on the expanse of my belly, and then he went lower to where my panties laid against my skin, right underneath my bellybutton.

His fingers teased the waistband. First, they went along the entire length, circling around one hip before they came back to the middle where the tiny pink bow lay. Then, the tip of one finger dipped below the waistline to run along the length of my pubic hair.

Over and over, just barely teasing.

It was enough to set my body on fire.

"Dante," I whimpered.

I felt his bearded chin along my shoulder, and then his lips were on my skin. My neck.

My jaw.

He peppered my body with kisses as he tasted me, and I started to shiver.

My legs were rubbing together as I tried to alleviate the ache he was causing, and I licked my lips before I finally took the plunge and shoved my panties down my legs.

Once they were kicked off, I spread them wide and threw one leg over his hips.

The room around me was dark so I couldn't see anything. I could only feel.

But feeling was enough.

I felt more than enough, actually.

His hand hovered just at the apex of my thighs, his fingers digging into my skin as I practically willed him to move forward. Just another inch and his fingers would be where it ached the most.

I shifted my hips to hopefully help, but still, he didn't move.

His lips had frozen at my neck, and I bit my lip as I reached for his hand.

The moment my hand touched his, he shivered.

"Like this," I whispered to him as I guided his hand down.

The moment I felt that blunt finger of his touch my clit, I knew that I was going to come.

Which, apparently, was all the encouragement that Dante needed.

He took control then.

His lips caught my skin, and he sucked lightly.

His hand delved deeper until his finger rested at the entrance to my sex.

And, before I could tell him a single thing, he let that finger slip inside of me.

I was so wet from his ministrations, as well as the simple fact that the man behind me was Dante, that it was almost embarrassing.

He felt so good.

God, everything about him was perfect.

"Dante," I breathed.

Still he remained silent, but it didn't matter.

He was perfect.

His fingers were perfect.

His mouth was perfect.

Everything about him was perfect.

I reached behind me and started to feel.

He had pants on, but not his jeans. Sleep pants.

His sleep pants were doing barely anything to contain his raging erection, and when I pushed his pants and boxers down, his cock sprung free and slapped against my lower back with a meaty thud.

I shivered as my hand circled around him, and Dante growled.

"Fuck."

His strangled curse word was enough to encourage me to continue. I pumped him with my fist, relishing in the fact that he filled it to overflowing.

I'd been with two men in my life, and both of them had been a disappointment.

Dante wasn't even inside of me yet, and he'd already given me more than the other two men ever had.

"Dante, I need you."

"No more talking," he ordered as he rolled me over onto my back.

And then he was between my thighs, his mouth on mine.

Still, he was careful to keep his weight off of me, remembering without me having to remind him that I was still recovering.

Which made my heart beat faster than ever.

And then I felt his cock at my entrance.

I couldn't see a thing, but his mouth hovered over mine, letting me know without words that he was there.

Seconds after that realization, he filled me in one long, slow thrust.

His mouth stayed fused to mine, and we breathed in each other's breaths.

One thrust. Two thrusts. Three. Four. Five. Six.

And then I came.

I came so long and hard that I took him with me.

He followed me over the edge, and by the time I came to, the first rays of the morning sun started peeking through the blinds.

The blinds of Dante's bedroom window.

I was in Dante's bed.

Oh my God.

I was in Dante's bed!

Then I said something I never should have said.

"Dante... I love you."

I knew the moment I said it that I should've never put voice to those words.

He got squigged out even when I showed him too much affection. Why would I think telling him 'I love you' would be any different?

It wasn't. In fact, the reaction I received was worse. Much worse.

He looked over at me, and I knew I'd lost him. He was no longer there with me. Well, mentally anyway. Physically he was there. But the rest of him? Poof in a cloud of smoke.

Dante's short little fuse had been lit, and in a matter of seconds, everything was blown to smithereens.

"Dante..."

"I need you to leave."

He yanked out of me so fast that I gasped in surprise.

"You what?"

He threw my panties and pants at my face.

"I need you to leave."

I took them, clutching them to my chest, and sat up.

"Why?"

He wouldn't look at me.

"Because I don't want you here."

"But…"

"I. Don't. Want. You. Here."

"You don't want me here." I sounded like a broken record. I couldn't find the words. I literally felt like I was floundering in water. Drowning. Was my head above water?

I literally felt sick to my stomach. Two minutes ago, I was on top of the world. And now… *well, now I wasn't sure how much lower I could be.*

"Okay," I said, sitting up and reaching down to slip my panties over my feet.

In the process, I leaked all down my leg and on his precious quilt. The one that he'd freaked out about when I'd used it to cover up here when I was first recovering.

The quilt he'd thrown away. The quilt that he'd seen after I'd washed it and immediately took to his room to lay over his bed. I hadn't seen it until today. Until he'd laid my head down next to it. It'd been only a glance. A short glance before he'd followed me down, placing his body on mine. Then I'd forgotten about everything but him. How he was making me feel.

And now, that feeling was nowhere in sight.

What was in sight was his release, which had come out of my vagina, dripping down on the quilt. I knew he'd seen it too because he flipped out. Again.

"Dante…"

"GET OUT!"

Yeah, I'd lost him. I haven't even really had him, and I lost him. Perfect. That was my life in a nutshell, though. A series of events that always ended up with me disappointed.

"Okay," I said quietly.

I dressed quietly. He watched me the whole time, anger in his eyes.

By the time I was leaving, I didn't think it could get much worse, but yet again, I was wrong.

"You were an obligation."

I froze, my hand on the knob.

That shatter I just heard? Yeah, that was my heart breaking into a million, tiny pieces.

I backed up, pulled open the door, and left without another word. Or at least, I tried to. But Dante, always so thorough, made sure to deliver the killing blow as I opened the door to my car.

"Never would've had anything to do with you had she not forced me. Extracted that promise from me on her deathbed."

And that, folks, is how to finish the destruction of a woman's heart. He completed the process by stomping on all of those shards that lay there from his first comments.

I turned, my foot half in my car, and let him see the devastation in my eyes.

"I should've just gone ahead and died like I wanted to. At least then I wouldn't have known how it felt to have someone you thought you cared about and could count on, say things meant to break you. Congratulations. You've officially made me wish I had cancer again. Hope that makes you feel good."

His eyes changed. But before I could listen to his nasty reply, I dropped all the way down into my car and slammed the door. Seconds later, I pulled out of his driveway... and his life.

***

Dante

The moment she left I knew I'd made a mistake. Hell, the moment I'd said the words I knew they were a mistake.

Yet, I'd still said them.

My heart, what remained of it, felt like it was suddenly gone. Not broken... *gone*.

I was glad to know that Mary, who'd been picked up while Cobie was napping earlier, was with my mother, safe and sound. Because the minute I saw Cobie drive away, tears coursing down her cheeks, I lost it.

I felt raw. Broken. Torn apart and shredded.

If it could get any worse, I'd probably accomplish it.

My knees hit the wood floor. The stupid, goddamned wood floor that had seen a thousand steps.

A thousand crawls. A hundred spills. Countless tears, and a few tantrums.

And I let one loose, too.

Why?

Because I knew I'd just made the stupidest mistake of my life. Nothing would ever be worse.

***

After composing myself, I went to her home, forgoing my usual route for expedience as I stopped in front of her place.

Only, she wasn't there like I'd expected.

Somebody else was, though.

Somebody who was just as pissed off as I was, only he was better prepared.

I felt the blow to my face and had one thought.

It was good Drake had caught me off guard. That would be the only way he'd accomplish what he set out to do next.

CHAPTER 21

Bite me.

-Things not to say to your captor

Dante

30 days in captivity

"You think you can take everything I have away from me?"

He hit me again.

Drake was a sick motherfucker.

We'd been doing this same old song and dance for thirty fucking days now.

I knew it was thirty days due to the fact that he'd conveniently left me a fucking calendar.

Each day he'd walk in, put a big red X through the previous day, and then walk into my cell.

My cell where I could just barely stretch arm to arm if I held them out wide. The cell itself was about six feet wide by six feet long.

He was even considerate enough to give me a pot to piss (and yes, shit) in.

I was chained at my feet and wrists, and if I wanted to do anything other than sit on my ass, it either hurt one or the other. They were long enough for me to stand hunched over, but not long enough for me to do much else.

Everything was raw, and every muscle in my body was sore from sitting here, scrunched up, for the last month. I was still in the same damn clothes I'd driven to Cobie's house in, but they were so dusty and dirty that they'd be thrown away if I ever got the fuck out of here.

At least it was cool and dry.

That's all I could say about this godforsaken mess that I found myself in.

The next blow came to my sternum, and it took me thirty seconds at least to find my breath after he delivered it.

I coughed and then smiled. "You ever going to let me go?"

"No," Drake snarled. "Because you've cost me a fuck load of money, and I'm not letting you go until you figure out a way to replace it."

"They're looking for me, you know."

Drake sneered.

"I know," he growled. "I have cameras all over this facility."

"What facility?"

"I wasn't just fucking around while Marianne was gone. I was building a fortress using stuff I acquired from my new friends. Cobie let me stay in her house, and during that time I had a few alterations made to her property."

"What kinds of alterations?"

"The kinds where I don't have to be in the main house to still be 'on the property.'"

The kinds that meant he'd been there all along, and we were probably still there.

I was being looked for, but it was highly unlikely I'd ever be found.

In the past thirty days, I'd had a lot of time to think.

A lot of time to contemplate my life.

And a lot of time to plan.

There were a few things that I was more than sure about.

One, I wanted to hold Mary again.

Two, I wanted to make up with my family. I wanted to forget the past, remember the good times that I had with my children and wife, but not live for just them anymore.

Three, I wanted to marry Cobie. I wanted her in my life. No, I *needed* her in my life.

I said some pretty nasty things to her because I'd felt guilty about how much happiness I'd felt while having her. There were feelings running through me that I hadn't even felt with my wife—which had been the real kicker in the guilt department. I wasn't supposed to love anyone else more than I loved my wife—but I did. I loved Cobie. I loved her with my whole heart and soul… and distance wouldn't change that.

I don't know how she snuck in there, but she had.

I was forty-one fucking years old. I most certainly had a good life with my wife and kids while it lasted. I hadn't needed anything else—or so I thought.

But I did need something else.

I needed someone to take care of. Someone to love me. Someone to love my Mary.

And Cobie did… she loved us.

Sometime while taking care of her over that six-week period, she'd stolen my heart. She'd shown me that there was something more to life than what I was giving it... and I hated that I'd thrown it all away because I'd been scared of those feelings that I was having.

But, if I was being honest, I was scared to lose those feelings again.

It was better—at least I thought at the time—to lose her now than to really let her get under my skin, and then lose her. But, she's already under my skin, so that's a moot point.

Even now, one month after she'd stormed out of my life pissed off at me, I was still feeling the burn of each one of the tears I'd seen fall down her face.

And I was certain, that as soon as I got out of this hell hole, I was going to make her mine. I was going to apologize.

I was going to marry that girl.

She just didn't know it yet.

***

61 days captive

I'd lost a lot of weight.

I was also very fucking tired of living on bread and water.

I craved a steak like never before, and I missed my family. One that was officially mine—Mary—and one that wasn't—Cobie.

But she would be... soon.

If only I could get out of here.

"You're not listening to me."

I felt the whip lash against my skin, but I didn't even feel it anymore.

Nope, not me.

Seriously, if there ever came a time when I did feel it, I'd be happy.

Why?

Because that would mean that I'd be on the way to healing.

There were open wounds on my back that started the first day that Drake took me, and today, he continued to reopen each and every one.

"You know what else is funny?"

I gritted my teeth.

"I can't find her."

My brows rose, and my head, which had been hanging, lifted.

"You think that's good, don't you?"

I nodded once.

"It's not."

"Why?" I rasped.

Was that really my voice?

I sounded like a newborn kitten.

"Because if I can't find her soon, they'll start looking for her."

"Why?" I asked.

I sounded like a fuckin' parrot, but my goddamn heart was slamming against the wall of my chest as I waited for him to answer, and I couldn't form a coherent thought.

"They think she's mine."

And then he smiled.

I wanted to kick him in the front teeth, but I couldn't even raise my leg far enough to do a goddamn thing, let alone kick him in the face.

My foot twitched, and he started to laugh.

Laugh it up, motherfucker. You're going to eat my heel one day, I'm goddamned sure of it.

***

94 days captive

He'd unhooked the chains from the wall, but not my wrists, thinking I was too weak to fight back.

I was... *mostly.*

But I knew that if he came close to me, I was going to kill him.

Today was the day he 'cleaned my cage' according to him.

And normally it happened once every few weeks. It'd been longer than that... I think.

Luckily, he'd fed me a decent meal yesterday because I was now feeling that extra energy.

I could practically taste the victory in the air.

It was about to go down.

I knew it.

Drake, though, acted oblivious as he started to spray the water over not just the cell I was in, but also me.

The feel of running water was enough to make me shiver.

I was down, in my guestimations, about thirty to forty pounds... if not more.

I felt weak as a kitten, but the closer and closer he came to me, the more intense the feeling inside of me grew.

Today. Was. The. Day.

The next step he took brought the bright red hose close to my face, and I moved until my body lay on top of it.

When he felt the resistance, he tugged.

I used his surprise and his imbalance against him. He turned and started to yank on the hose again. I used his inattention at his back to my advantage and swept my foot out.

His foot caught on the chain and he fell.

His hands went out to catch his fall, but I moved fast—or as fast as I could, anyway.

He came down to the ground, and I wasted no time wrapping the chain that was attached to my wrist around his throat. Then, for good measure, I brought the hose up and shoved it down his throat.

He sputtered, choked and fought.

Water was going everywhere, not just down his throat.

He was gasping. I was gasping.

My arms and legs burned.

He went limp after about five seconds.

I held him for a little bit longer…then let him go.

Not because I didn't want to make sure the fucker was actually dead—but because I physically couldn't hold it anymore.

I fell to the ground, completely and utterly spent, panting as I tried to find the ability to move.

The only thing I could accomplish was reaching for the phone that I knew Drake always kept in his perfectly-starched dress pants.

I found it.

Then groaned when I realized that there was a password on it.

FUCK!

But then I smiled as I looked over at Drake's hand.

Thank God for the geniuses at Apple. One way around the password protection was the fingerprint feature. Seeing as I had the access to those fingers and their prints via their unconscious, and hopefully dead, owner's hand, it wouldn't be a problem for me to get into his phone.

After trying, and then wiping Drake's thumb dry on the only dry part on his shirt, I gained access to the iPhone.

I didn't call 911. I called Rafe.

***

Three weeks later

It took me almost a month to gain back *some* of my lost weight, for my wounds to be treated and begin to heal and for me to find the fucking will to live. Two of those days I spent in and out of consciousness as my body tried to find a way to heal the damage that had been done to it.

Then, I became totally aware.

And when I became aware, I was in pain.

Pain that I relished.

In those three weeks, I hadn't been feeling well enough at any given time to do a goddamn thing. Until today.

"Just listen to me, goddammit." Travis hauled me back by my wrist. "You're not ready to just go charging out there after him."

I narrowed my eyes.

"I'm not charging after him," I snapped. "I've been working with the therapists. I'm getting stronger. I'm going to grab a hamburger, some fries, check on Mary…and then find my woman."

Travis's mouth closed. "You're not going after him?"

I shook my head. "No."

Travis was scared I was going after him because, in the hustle and bustle of Rafe finding me, the police coming in, and them trying to save me—because, apparently, the exertion from my fight with Drake was too much on my already weakened and overtaxed heart, and I'd passed out—Drake had escaped.

According to Rafe, Drake wasn't there when he'd arrived.

I couldn't tell you, because after placing the phone call to Rafe, the last thing I remember was feeling like something was twisting every muscle in my body. Then I must have passed out.

"Remember, you're not supposed to overexert yourself."

I waved my hand in a vague sweeping motion. "I'll be fine."

"You will not be fine!" my mother snapped.

I ignored her, as well as the rest of my brothers, and kept walking.

Today was the day.

CHAPTER 22

*If you're going to fuck something up, fuck it all
kinds of up.*

Cobie

Present day

Snick.

Frowning, I looked around the kitchen to see nothing out of the
ordinary.

However, that was usual. I'd been hearing a lot of strange noises
lately… noises that made me freak way the fuck out. Yet, each
time I had gotten up to investigate, nothing was there.

I looked over to my kitty that was still laying just as peacefully as
he'd been laying hours before, and snorted.

"You're hearing things again," I said to myself.

My kitty, Yum-Yum, raised his head, blinking at me sleepily.

"Oh, did I wake you from your nap, Yum-Yum?"

He laid his head back down and resumed his previous position, not
giving me the time of day.

I snorted.

Then I looked around the old, unfamiliar house that wasn't mine and sighed.

Old houses made a lot of noises that couldn't be explained. Floors creaking, wood shifting in the wind, strange cracks appearing and disappearing in the walls when the heat of the day left for the cool of night. Seriously, I should be used to it seeing as I lived in my own house as old as time. Yet I wasn't. Why, you ask?

Because with every single creak and groan I heard, I prayed that it was signaling the return of that stupid man who I stupidly loved. God, I was so stupid. Stupid, stupid, stupid.

I loved him. I understood. But I was still so mad at him.

I pounded the dough one more time with a tight fist, then growled in frustration.

"Stupid man," I hissed. "Stupid, non-ugly, beautiful-looking-but-ugly-talking, always right, caring father, never going to let me have my way, no good, son of a bitch, asshole, fucking jerkface, stupid…"

"You already said stupid."

I looked up from my dough and gasped.

Dante. In my house.

Standing directly in front of me.

"How did you get in here?" I snarled, squeezing the dough in my fist. "More importantly, how did you find me?"

He was standing across the kitchen island from me, staring at me with something I couldn't quite decipher in his eyes.

"I walked through the front door. You shouldn't leave it unlocked."

I narrowed my eyes. "The front door wasn't open."

I knew for a fact that it wasn't unlocked because I'd been preparing for this possibility. Thinking about it, hoping for it, and praying that it would come, yet still scared that it might actually happen, and I'd have to face him. I'd have to see him, in the flesh, as I tried to work through the anger and sadness that still continued to pour through me.

He shrugged. "Took me a while to find you."

I blinked.

I'd hidden well.

So well, in fact, that it took him four months to find me—at least I prayed that was the reason that he'd taken so long.

Then again, the fact that I was well hidden was mostly due to Rafe. He'd taken one look at my pitiful self, handed me a set of keys, a thousand dollars in cash, and gave me directions to one of his homes that was out of state.

Out of state in Ala-freakin'-bama.

One of his homes. I'd asked him how many he had. He said twelve. *Twelve.*

I wasn't really sure how Dante had found me, but my guess was that Rafe had given him the information. There was literally no other way, not with where I was located.

I hadn't left my little bubble in a very long time. When I did have to leave, I was hyper-vigilant.

I stepped away from the counter, hands covered in bits of dough and flour, and turned quickly for the sink.

My shirt was covered with flour also, and without thinking, I swiped at a stray fleck and then winced.

Now I had even more there. Great.

And then I realized that not only was I wearing a very tight tank top, but it was also showing off my non-existent chest, as well as the other thing I'd been hiding with the countertop.

"When were you going to tell me?"

I shrugged, instead focusing on washing my hands instead of the man that had rounded the counter.

"*Were* you going to tell me?"

I shrugged again. "Eventually."

"When eventually?" he persisted.

"When I was damn good and ready."

"Maybe when you weren't pregnant anymore?" He moved. "When you were having the kid? When she was eighteen?"

I shivered at his close proximity.

"He." I licked my lips.

"He who?"

I looked at him like he was stupid.

"He as in our *son*."

He froze.

"Son?"

I nodded once. "Son."

Then, the big man before me started to cry. Not small tears either. Big, fat, rib-crushing tears.

He hit his knees, and his head dropped. His shoulders shook with his big, racking sobs.

And that's when I knew the man I fell in love with was back.

He'd done whatever thinking he'd needed to do.

I didn't doubt that he'd find me again. I knew he would.

Did I think it'd take him four months to get his head on straight? *No.* I thought it'd take him a couple of days.

But, he was here.

I hoped.

"I'm so sorry."

I didn't know what to say or do.

He was down on his knees. He was still sobbing, and I frowned when I saw his hands that came up to curve around his neck.

They were scarred.

What?

He had a large red gash along his right forearm, one that looked like he'd whipped it against a tree limb or something. It was raised, red, and angry.

He was also wearing a… *hospital bracelet?*

"Dante," I said, touching the bracelet. "Did you hurt yourself?"

He didn't answer, instead he got to his feet.

"I've done a lot of things in my life that I'm not proud of, but over the last four months, I've had a lot of time to think." He laughed humorlessly at whatever thoughts were going through his head. Something that I wasn't privy to yet. "I've gone through hell twice in my life. Once when I lost my first wife and kids, and then again when I lost you and Mary…"

"What do you mean you lost Mary?"

He spoke over me.

"…and every day of these last four months was a lesson in control that I realized I didn't have. There have been two people in my life that have reduced me to a befuddled mess. Lily… and you. Lily's not here anymore, but you are. It took me a while to realize, to understand what I felt and to give myself permission to accept what you were offering me. I didn't recognize that what we have is that rare, once-in-a-lifetime, forever kind of love until you left. I didn't know how much you meant to me until I felt your pain and saw the hurt I put in your eyes. I never, ever want to experience that again."

I didn't know what to say.

"I know you don't know what to say," he stopped. "And you may think that this is just about the baby, now that I know we're having him, but you'd be wrong. I'm gonna love that boy no matter what. But you… I can't live without you. I don't want to live without you."

Tears were streaming down my cheeks unchecked, and I continued to look into the eyes of the man that I knew I loved.

"I never once doubted your love for me, Dante," I said softly, raising one hand to his overly scruffy cheek. "At least, not after I had time to think. I knew you were coming to terms with things in your head. What I did doubt was the timing. I wasn't sure if we were happening at the right time or if we were in the same place emotionally for it. But I was willing to wait, to give you that time… at least until it was time to bring this kid into the world."

His eyes softened, and the tears slowed. His, not mine.

Once mine started, it was very hard to get them to stop.

"Your cancer scares me."

I knew that, too.

The possibility of him losing someone he loved, this time to a nasty disease, had to be overwhelming for him. He'd already lost so much… I'm sure it was taking everything he had to even be here.

I knew that.

"I can't promise you I'll be here forever."

His eyes dropped to my chest.

"Is everything okay?"

I pressed on my chest, then went farther to gather the ends of my shirt.

Taking a deep breath, I raised it up and over my head.

His breath caught. But his eyes weren't on my surgical scars. They were on my belly.

My perfectly rounded belly that was just starting to stick out.

It was cute, even I thought so. I was just past that stage where people were wondering whether I was getting fat or if I was actually pregnant. Now it was obvious that I was pregnant.

He raised his hand and ran it along my belly. His whole palm spanned the entire width of my baby bump.

"Can you feel him yet?"

I nodded.

"From the outside?"

I shook my head.

And then, as if to give me a taste of things to come, our son proved me wrong and did just that—he kicked.

So hard, in fact, that Dante felt it.

It was little. Dante probably felt nothing more than a slight flutter against his palm, but he sucked in a deep breath in response.

His chest rose, and it was then that I started to take stock of his appearance.

He looked rough… really rough.

His eyes were dark, the bags under them a deep purple. His beard was scruffier than I'd ever seen it, and his lips were chapped and cracked. Pairing that with the state of his arms, and the way he'd looked to have lost twenty pounds if the state of his clothes which were hanging on him were anything to go by, he wasn't in any better shape than I had been over the last few months.

Then he dropped his mouth to my belly, his hands running up the back of my thighs.

And that was all that I needed.

My body went from caring to wanting in about two point seven seconds. I'd thought about him so much over the last few months that it was downright comical. I'd had one sexual encounter with this man, but it was enough to give me an idea of what I was missing.

And I used that sexual encounter, right down to the last itty-bitty detail, and replayed it in my mind as I did the dirty deed every night in the dark of my borrowed bedroom.

I shivered in Dante's arms, and it only took one half of a second for me to be up and off my feet.

He had his arms locked around my hips as he carried me out of the kitchen and to the only other room in the small cabin—the bedroom.

He kicked the door farther open, took slow steps toward the bed, and laid me down gently.

He didn't throw me, didn't let me bounce. No, he placed me so softly on the bed that I almost started crying again right then and there—as if he was scared he was going to break me.

"I've missed you so much."

I would've responded, but he crawled up my body and placed his lips on mine.

I couldn't help but respond to this man.

His hands skimmed the naked skin of my side, trailing lightly upward to my arms. Once he had them both in his large palms, he pushed them up and over my head.

Then he moved his mouth down, trailing his beard along the skin of my jaw.

He kissed me behind my ear. On my collarbone.

Then stopped to hover between the scars on my chest.

"You're beautiful," he rasped, dipping out his tongue to trail down the center of my chest to the soft swell of my belly.

He hovered there for a few long moments before letting my arms go to allow him to move even farther down to the waistband of my yoga pants.

He then crawled up between my knees.

His eyes lifted to mine as he started to pull my pants down my legs—which got stuck around mid-thigh due to his body between my splayed thighs.

He lifted my legs straight up into a ninety-degree angle and pulled them the rest of the way off.

As my legs started to move back down toward the bed, he caught them behind my knees, hooking his arms around my legs and pulling me into position with my backside resting against his knees.

His hot eyes on me made me feel a thousand miles tall. So obviously full of lust for me, despite my lack of breasts and my scars, things I didn't have any chance of hiding from him.

"God, you're so beautiful."

Before I could start crying, his mouth was back on mine.

I dove into the kiss, my need for him a living, breathing thing that wouldn't be satisfied. Not now, not ever.

"Dante," I gasped as I pulled away.

He moved to my neck, sucking lightly.

I moaned and flexed my legs, trapping his biceps between my calves and the backs of my thighs on each side. "Dante, please. I just... I just need."

He let go of my neck with a soft suck that seemed to echo off the walls of the tiny room and then pulled back to look at me.

His eyes took me in—my disheveled hair, the scars on my chest, and then my belly.

"I don't want to hurt you."

I knew that he was talking about more than sex now.

"Then don't."

His eyes flashed, and he smiled. "I won't, not ever again. I'll treat you like you deserve."

He dropped one of his hands to pull at the waistband of his jeans.

His shirt and jeans stayed on, but his cock sprung out through that gap in his jeans that unbuttoning had created.

He wasn't wearing any underwear.

I smiled.

"I won't ever hurt you again."

And then he leaned forward, one of my legs still in the crook of his arms, as he notched the head of his cock to my entrance.

My eyes held his as he pushed slowly inside. My slick wetness eased the way, and he didn't even have to pull back as he forged his way inside. One slow, smooth inch at a time, until he was buried inside of me to the hilt.

I felt full—so freakin' full.

It was one of the best feelings in the world.

Looking into his eyes, watching him take me, was probably the single most intimate moment I have ever experienced. Not that I'd ever allow anybody else to know what it was like to be watching this man in the same way. He was mine.

He thrust deep into me and stilled.

I arched my back, looking for more.

"What's that look for?"

I smiled, then dropped one of my hands to gather some of the moisture that had collected around the base of his cock.

"Oh, nothing." I smiled as I dragged that moisture up to where I needed it most—my clit.

He pulled back and watched me play for a few long moments before he slowly sank back inside.

I slowed the swirls that my fingers were drawing on my clit to match his pace. One swirl, then a thrust.

One swirl, then a thrust.

I stopped when I felt my orgasm getting close.

I didn't want to go yet, not when it felt this good—this right.

I'd never, ever felt anything that would ever compare to this moment in time.

He watched me watch him, our eyes staying connected for long minutes.

Sweat started to drip down his face, but he still continued his slow pace.

I could feel the head of his cock kiss the entrance to my womb with each plunge, and I suddenly realized that whether I was playing with my clit or not, he was going to make me come.

And then he balanced all of his weight on one arm and reached for the hand that was touching my clit minutes before.

He brought my fingers up to his mouth, and then sucked them into his mouth, one at a time.

My pussy clenched, my back arched… and I came.

It was all I needed.

By sheer force of will, I managed to keep my eyes open and watch him through it. It was one of the hardest things I'd ever done in my life. But the way he watched me and then followed me over moments later? I'd have that memory buried deep for the rest of my life.

I actually felt the pulse of his cock as he came, shooting himself inside of me. Once. Twice. Three times.

And then he stilled.

Our breathing was uneven, but he didn't waver in his eye contact.

"I love you back, Cobie," he whispered. "I'll never, not ever, take that for granted again."

And then I started to cry all freakin' over again.

***

It was an hour later, my rescued dough was in the oven turning into a wonderful, delicious smelling bread when I broached the subject.

Dante was busy shoveling food down his throat, partaking in my mad baking skills—skills that only made themselves known when

I was stressed. He was on his fourth chocolate chip cookie when I finally found the nerve to ask.

"What took you so long?" I whispered, pouring milk into a glass for him and studiously gazing at it instead of giving him the eye contact that I was sure he wanted.

When he didn't say anything, I finally looked up to see him staring at me.

His eyes changed from sorrow to calculation.

Was he trying to gauge my gumption?

I stiffened my spine and gave him my full, undivided attention.

"What?"

He licked his lips, and then scratched behind his ear.

"I would have found you three and a half months ago… but… stuff came up."

My mouth dropped open. "And you just left me here to wallow in self-pity? All this time?"

His lips twitched at my outrage. Was he amused by this?

"Drake decided to make a move after you left."

My mouth fell open.

"You're joking."

He winced. "No, not joking. Not even a little bit."

"What did he do…"

And then Dante dropped his half-eaten cookie, stood from his stool, and rounded the counter.

"I'm okay."

I frowned. "Well, I noticed."

"No, I'm okay. I don't want you to freak out."

"Okay…"

He stopped a foot or so away from me and started to lift his shirt.

I gasped.

The marks on his arms weren't the only thing new.

I could see his ribs. He had abs, of course, but Dante had always been thick and muscular. Now I could see all of his fucking ribs.

And then he turned…

"Oh my God." I started to reach out but froze mid-air. "Oh, God. Oh, God. Dante… what happened?"

His back was a mess of the same little lesions that were on his arms and hands… only they were so much worse, it was downright terrifying.

While we were making love, I'd felt the ridges underneath his T-shirt, of course.

But my body had been so focused on him… on what I was feeling… that it never registered on me that what I was feeling were actually wounds.

I'd thought, at the time, that they were just part of his T-shirt.

They weren't.

"Dante," the gasp left my throat. "What… what *is* that?"

He turned and stared. "Whip marks."

"Whip marks?"

"Yes."

"How…"

This wasn't computing. Why would Dante stand still long enough to get those marks on his back. And they weren't even all the way on his back. Now that I paid more attention to his front, they were on the side of his neck. His ribs. They even circled around his hips and curled around to his front. Down his pants.

What. The. Hell?

"When you left, Drake found me."

"And he smacked you around with a whip, and you let him by just standing there?"

I really wasn't seeing how this could happen…

"No, he caught me off guard." He paused. "I was outside your house. My mind was fucked up. I couldn't stop thinking about what I'd said to you—which I'm still fucked up about, by the way—and I wasn't paying attention to my surroundings. Something hit me in the back of the head—they said it was probably a two-by-four—and when I woke up, I was in a cell underneath your old house."

In a cell. *Underneath my old house?*

"For how long?" I whispered, my eyes closing in despair.

"For three and a half months."

My eyes opened as a keening cry of utter despair left my mouth. "Three and a half months. And what did he do to you in those three and a half months?"

I was almost afraid to hear the rest.

Every night I had cursed him. I had been so freakin' mad at him for not getting his head on straight faster, I couldn't fucking think.

And all of this time… all of this time he'd been in a cell. A freakin' cell. Being beaten.

"He whipped me. Tortured me. Starved me and humiliated me."

"What did he do?"

Dante shook his head. "I won't be telling you specifics."

I wanted to argue. I wanted to rage.

But I could see the resolve in his eyes.

He wouldn't be telling me.

That I knew.

"How did you finally get away?"

What would he have had to do? If he'd been there for that long, then surely nobody could find him. Right?

"Drake got careless. Thought I was too weak to move—which was what he'd planned by only feeding me a slop and a slice of bread morning, noon and night. But one day while he was hosing out the cell to combat the smell, he got too close, and I struck. I choked him with the chains he had me—"

"Chains!"

"—held down with, and fed him the water he was using to spray me with. Once he went limp, I found his phone and called Rafe. The rest is still a blur. I don't really remember what happened next."

I couldn't breathe.

Dante wrapped his arms around my shoulders and pulled me in tight to his chest.

"I'm okay."

"You're not okay."

I could feel those raised scars underneath my fingers.

He was not *okay.*

"What about since you got away from him?" I whispered. "Were you in the hospital?"

He nodded.

"Drake got away. That's why they didn't call you to come."

I nodded, throat thick with guilt.

I should've never left him.

And I told him as much.

"I needed you to leave," he rasped. "If you hadn't left, I wouldn't have realized what I was missing. Without you, I wouldn't have realized just how sad and bleak my life had become."

I made another of those sounds in the back of my throat.

"He forgot to tell you about his problems stemming from his captivity."

I froze in Dante's arms, just as Dante cursed and let me go.

My eyes lit on Rafe in the entrance.

"What?"

Rafe's eyes flicked from mine to Dante's and back. "He has a muscle-wasting condition called rhabdomyolysis. The exertion from the fight, paired with his overtaxed heart—his dehydration, his lack of food, as well as the wounds on his body—could cause a heart attack. He was supposed to be taking it easy. He was supposed to be letting *me* come get you."

Dante didn't say a word.

I did, though.

"You mean to tell me that you're supposed to be taking it easy, and you just had sex with me? That wasn't taking it easy! There was nothing easy about it!" I semi-shrieked into Dante's ear.

Dante pulled me into his chest again.

"Oh, I don't know about that, it was pretty easy getting you into bed." His grin was wide.

I hit him and then apologized before kissing the tiny hurt I must've just caused him.

"I'll be okay," he promised. "I *am* okay. Those circumstances aren't going to happen again."

I swallowed the bile that was making its way up my throat—a common occurrence as of late.

This bile felt differently, though.

I just knew that I was going to puke, so I took off toward the bathroom and lost what little lunch that I'd had left in me from earlier in the toilet.

"Rafe knew you were gone all this time, didn't he?"

I looked over my shoulder to see Rafe.

"Yeah," Dante croaked at the same time Rafe nodded his head.

Even his voice sounded different.

I lost my battle with the tears, and I dissolved.

Jesus Christ. I was a broken record today.

CHAPTER 23

The struggle bus should have a loyalty program.

-Dante's secret thoughts

Dante

"Ummm." Cobie looked around the place. "What happened?"

We'd just arrived home—to my home—after a very long drive.

We were only coming to pick up some clothes, and then I was picking Mary up and we were heading back to Cobie's place.

I would have cleaned up, but the moment I was released from the hospital I'd gone to check on Mary. Once I knew she was okay, I'd left her with Reed and his wife, and then I immediately left for Alabama, where Rafe had stashed Cobie.

I'd been so fucking mad—still—that I'd lashed out without thought. A-fucking-gain. I was good at that, though. It was the apologizing part that I wasn't good at.

I looked around the house, seeing the broken light fixture that Lily had bought and lovingly restored. Her prized China that we'd gotten as a gift on our wedding day from my mother was shattered into tiny pieces. The stupid Tupperware that was always in perfect order, tossed haphazardly across the room.

Then I came to the living room. The sofa—the one that Lily had begged and pleaded with me to get despite the ugly flowers—was shredded, courtesy of my hunting knife. The same knife that had also been taken to the drapes. Those stupid goddamn drapes that I freakin' hated.

Cobie moved into the hallway that led to the bedrooms and stopped when she saw all the open doors.

I hadn't touched the girls' rooms. Which she noticed as she walked past. Not Mary's. Not My other two lost girls. My bedroom, though? The one I shared with Lily?

Yeah, that room was the worst.

I braced as she turned the corner and paused in the doorway before she moved a little bit farther into the room.

She inched her way in, her head swinging from side-to-side, eyes wide and horrified as they took in the scene before her, and finally came to a stop in the center of the bedroom. I saw the stupid bed that Lily refused to retire—even after we could afford something new—now in about thirty jagged pieces on the floor. The mattress was also in shreds, thanks again to the same hunting knife that I'd used on the drapes and sofa.

The same knife that was now planted in the wall right through a picture. One that I loved but Lily had hated.

It was a picture of the Hostel skyline. Our business was in the background, the main focus had been the tow truck. The older-than-dirt truck that had more dents and dings in it than it had smooth spots. The paint was faded and chipped, the body had rust crusting along the bottom of the frame, and the tires looked like they needed replacing about six months before the picture had been taken. But I'd been standing in front of it, happy as fucking hell to have my first business.

I'd been thirty years old. Fresh out of the military. Married. There was trash strewn all around me from a festival the night before, and Lily disliked seeing all the trash. But me? I didn't care one bit. In that moment, I was on top of the world.

Happy. So fucking happy.

"What happened?"

"I decided to do a little redecorating."

That's when Cobie started to laugh.

And that's also when my control snapped. I didn't want to be away from her anymore. I wanted her to be in my arms.

Therefore, I made it so.

I reached forward, snagged her by her tee, and tugged her to me.

She came willingly.

"What?"

I didn't answer for a moment as I stared down into her eyes. I leaned forward slowly so she knew what my intentions were. "This."

Then I kissed her. I kissed her long and sweet and thorough. She tasted like second chances, salvation and starting over. I never wanted to let her go.

Not ever again.

We had so much to talk about, and there were so many things she needed to know.

But right then and there? Nothing else mattered but us and that moment, and the way her body felt against mine.

I had only intended for it to be a quick kiss—short and sweet.

But as it seemed to be the way with everything about Cobie, it quickly turned into something more. Something softer and sweeter.

"We can't," she whispered.

My dick didn't care if I shouldn't. It only cared that she was in my arms again after months of wanting and needing her.

"We can," I said. "If you do all the work."

Then I was on the floor, her straddling my waist.

She shook her head, still unsure. "I don't know…"

I lifted my shirt up and off my body, then started in on my pants.

"My dick is fine," I told her, showing her.

It sprang free of my pants.

"Your mom's going to be here in twenty minutes…"

I arched up, rubbing my dick against the apex of her thighs.

She stopped her protests and gave in. That easily.

Moments later she was standing over me, stripping the leggings from her frame, followed shortly by her panties.

Then she was back on top of me, guiding herself onto my cock.

In one swift movement, I held my cock up, and she lowered herself down on top of it.

I closed my eyes as she took me.

Chaos ruled our world at the moment. My house was a goddamn mess, and my body wasn't much better.

But this, right here, her wet heat wrapped around me? Yeah, that was nothing short of perfection.

"Ride me," I ordered.

And like the good girl Cobie was, she did just that.

She took me, over and over again, until we were both on the peak.

I pressed my finger against her clit, and that was all she wrote.

She came and brought me with her.

Then we laid there like broken dolls until I heard my mother walk in my front door.

"We gotta get up."

"Dada!"

And that was my cue.

I got up, but not before dropping a soft kiss on Cobie's upturned lips.

Cobie smiled, and I knew then that I'd be going to the jewelry store tomorrow.

I needed to buy this woman a ring and get it on her finger. Once she accepted it, I'd make sure she never forgot how much I loved her every day for the rest of our lives.

And she would accept it.

I'd make sure of that, too.

***

Cobie came down the stairs long minutes later, and she smiled the moment she saw Mary.

"Mary, Mary!" Cobie cooed, holding out her hands for Mary.

Mary ditched me like a piece of burnt toast, squealing when Cobie brought her into her arms.

"That's adorable," my mother whispered.

I lifted my arm and wrapped it around my mother's shoulders.

"It is," I agreed.

We stayed silent as we listened to the two of them chatter on and on about this and that. Half of the words I wasn't even sure that Cobie even understood, but she didn't let on.

She nodded her head, held eye contact, and then laughed.

My mother patted my belly.

"Are you going to make an honest woman out of her?"

My mother didn't miss much.

Certainly not a pregnancy that would bring her another grandchild.

"Yeah," I confirmed. "As soon as she'll accept me."

My mother patted my belly one more time. "Honestly, Dante. You are one of the cutest boys. You have nothing to worry about."

I snorted, and the movement caused my back to twinge.

Cobie looked over at me, gestured toward the living room, and I nodded.

I swallowed as I tried not to think about the pain I was still in, and instead focused on my mother.

"I'm sorry."

My mother stepped away from me and looked up.

"What for?"

"I spent a long time in a place that I wasn't sure that I could dig myself out of. I'm sorry that you had to suffer losing me, too."

My mother's eyes filled with tears, and I instantly saw the wariness. She looked older than her years, and I wondered when that had happened.

Probably when I was busy pushing everyone away.

"Honey," my mother said. "I've suffered a lot of loss in my life. I've lost your sisters. A daughter-in-law. Three grandchildren. But

I still have the man that is the other half of my soul. I still have six of my kids. I still have a lot of grandkids, and now some new daughters, thanks to your brothers marrying. I know that you had to fight your own battles. I knew it, and I understood it. You were there when we needed you most, and that was enough until you were ready to come back to me. But the three months that you were gone? I don't want to feel like that again. So, if you could, try not to let that happen again, m'kay?"

I winked at my mother. "I'll see what I can do."

She patted my cheek. "Now, I'm going to go spend some alone time with your father. We haven't had a kidless bed for a few very long months."

I tried not to think about what they were going to do in that kidless bed as I said my goodbyes.

But I was glad that I'd apologized. I'd needed to do that for a while now, and I wasn't going to put off any more apologies. I never knew if today would be my last.

Which was why tomorrow I'd be proposing to that woman in my living room. I wanted to make her mine.

Because tomorrow may not dawn as bright as today did.

And I didn't want to regret a damn thing when the day was over.

CHAPTER 24

I'm lacking the 'zippity' part of my doo-dah day.

-Dante to Cobie

Dante

We were at another Uncertain Saints MC party.

I was asked to attend this one because it was one of the Little Saints birthday parties.

I'd avoided those parties like the plague because every single one of those motherfuckers were now married with kids. I'd gone the last time with Cobie on a whim. I'd been in no mood to deal with anyone or anything after that conversation with the stupid chick in the diner.

So, I just went for a ride. I found myself taking a familiar route, and I wound up at the Uncertain Saints clubhouse. A place that I never thought I'd willingly end up at ever again.

One of their members had been married to my sister.

And I'd hated him.

I'd hated him with a passion because he'd been in the process of divorcing my sister when she was killed. Though, my dislike of the man had died down after Wolf had found his new wife, Raven.

Raven had been the deciding factor in me trusting the man again, and while we hadn't become exactly close, I could at least tolerate him now.

In the past, the Hail House—our club that we'd opened a few years back—was off limits to them. After Wolf, Travis and I had repaired the breach between us, we'd gotten to the point where we now hung out with them occasionally—or at least Travis did. I hadn't had much to do with them seeing as not long after that breach was healed, my wife and children had died.

I'd been invited, but Wolf's calls had been ignored right along with the rest of my family's.

Until a few weeks ago.

I'd been back three times, one of those times with Cobie.

This time, though, Cobie was obviously pregnant.

She was also sporting a huge rock on her finger signaling she was mine and would be *legally* in just a few short weeks.

Plus, this time Mary would be introduced to them for the first time.

I hadn't brought her with me to many places. This would literally be the first time anyone besides close friends and family would meet this little girl—this amazing, sweet little girl who has become my whole world—and learn that she was mine.

My girl, Mary, was unique, and there would be a lot of kids there running around.

I knew that those kids were from good stock, but I didn't want them to hurt my baby's feelings.

"Dante, you need to chill."

I winced and realized what I was doing at once.

"Okay," I said as I unstrapped Mary from her car seat and hitched her up on my hip.

The first person to meet us was Griffin Storm, a badass Texas Ranger who looked like he was angry as fuck at something that his kid had just done.

"How many times do I have to tell you to stay away from my bike?" Griffin growled.

Cobie's hand met the skin of my arm, and she started to squeeze.

I patted her hand and assured her without words that everything was okay.

Griffin might talk a good game, but when it came to his kids, he was a sucker—just like the rest of us.

"Now, go inside and tell Mommy what you've done."

His kid ran inside moments later, and Griffin glared at her back until she'd made it inside and slammed the door.

"What happened?" I asked.

Griffin turned his angry eyes to me, and they moved from me to the little girl in my arms and then to Cobie. His eyes skimmed down Cobie's body, and then the glare slipped from his face as he caught sight of her baby bump.

"You have kids yet?" he asked the woman at my side.

"Only Mary."

I grinned at Cobie's words.

I loved that she claimed my girl as hers.

Fucking. Loved. It.

I waited for Griffin to ask more, but he didn't.

His eyes went to Mary.

"This Miss Mary?"

Mary, hearing her name, looked directly at Griffin.

And I watched the big man lose his heart just like every other person who looked into her big blue eyes.

Mary leaned over and practically threw herself into Griffin's arms.

Griffin caught her easily and hefted her up onto his arm just like I'd had her moments before.

"Yum-Yum?"

"Uhhh," Griffin said, looking to me for guidance.

"Yum-Yum is our cat," I said, tilting my head at the cat that'd magically appeared on top of Griffin's bike. "Every cat is now Yum-Yum to her."

Griffin turned and growled.

He picked the cat up by the scruff of the neck, then handed it to me. "Take this for me?"

I took the cat.

"What'd he do?" I looked down at what I thought to be a harmless cat.

"What hasn't he done is a better question," Griffin grumbled.

My eyes went down to the bike, which sported lengthy scratches on the gas tank that looked like they came from a particular cat that I might be holding.

I held back my grin.

Griffin sighed and gestured with his head for me to follow him.

"Might as well go inside and listen to the music."

We followed along, coming to a halt right inside the entrance as Griffin's daughter tearfully told her mother a story.

"And why was the kitty outside?" Lenore, Griffin's wife, asked. "We told you not to even bring him. Then you took him outside, didn't you?"

Griffin's daughter nodded her head.

"Then what happened?"

"He got on Daddy's bike, and I tried to pull him off. B-b-but, he scratched the paint when I did."

Lenore winced.

"You know that Daddy just got his bike repainted after you decorated it with your nail polish," Lenore chastised their girl gently.

I bit my lip and looked up at Griffin who looked far from amused, causing me to let out a low chuckle.

Lenore looked up at me then, and her eyes widened.

I was still rather emaciated looking, but I was slowly gaining my color as well as the weight back.

I'd been out of the hospital, and back with Cobie, for a week.

In that week, I'd been busy.

Since I was back at work, I took Mary with me.

It wasn't that I didn't trust my mother to watch her, it was because I didn't trust Drake not to attack an innocent little girl in his haste to get to me.

So, for now, where I went, she went.

At the office, Travis was always there to help. Half the time, Rafe was, too.

I had a feeling he expected Drake to come at me there, so instead of wasting his time trying to look for him—which proved futile since no one could find him at his usual haunts—he'd set up shop at the office and was waiting.

"You look like you've lost weight."

My eyes went back to Griffin's wife.

I nodded. "I have."

She didn't say what she was obviously thinking—'you look like shit.'

I knew I looked like shit, she didn't have to tell me.

"He's getting better," Cobie interjected. "Do you have a bathroom I could use?"

Griffin's little girl, happy to no longer be the center of attention, came at me with arms raised.

I handed her the cat, and she took off without another word.

Griffin and Lenore watched her go before they both turned back to Cobie.

"It's through here. Come on, I'll show you."

Lenore gestured to Cobie, and Cobie followed.

We waited until they were both gone before heading in the direction of where all the other men were gathered on the porch.

Griffin and I walked out onto the porch, and all eyes turned to us.

"Who ya got there, Griffin?"

Griffin tickled Mary, who giggled like a sweet, angelic cherub, completely winning over the deck full of men.

Wolf came up and held his hands out.

Mary went willingly.

"Trusting little booger."

I looked over to find Mig, another member of the Uncertain Saints, looking our way.

"She is. Never meets a stranger, that's for sure," I agreed.

Mig grunted and held out his hands, Mary leaned over.

I snorted as the men then passed my girl around.

None of them had anything to say about Mary's unique qualities.

Which made my heart fucking soar.

I didn't ever want Mary to feel like those things that made her different and special were oddities or things that she needed to hide or be ashamed of because they weren't. They were what made Mary, well, Mary, and she was perfect exactly as she was.

She was a blessing, a gift—*my gift*.

Mary had saved my life.

I'd fight every fucking demon on this planet to make sure she was never hurt by someone's cruel words.

Even a band full of men who I knew could kick my ass in my weakened state.

"Noticed you have a pregnant fiancée."

I looked over to Griffin, who'd said those words.

"Yeah," I agreed.

"How'd you manage to do that while you were locked away?"

I grunted. "One happened before I left. Found out after I got back."

"I hear you've got a few problems."

I grunted in reply.

"More than a few," I agreed, my eyes going to Wolf.

"I've been lookin' myself." Wolf read the look accurately. "If I see him, he's going down. That's a promise."

Wolf was a Texas Ranger with Griffin, and I had no doubt in my mind that he'd take him in if he saw him.

"Thanks," I muttered. "This feels really fuckin' weird, still."

Wolf chuckled darkly. "I keep waiting for you to throw another punch."

I would have five years ago.

Now? Well, now I wasn't as angry about it as I once had been. In fact, I wasn't angry at all anymore.

"The night is still young."

Wolf burst out laughing. "Sure the fuck is."

CHAPTER 25

*The only thing I will ever force in my life are my
jeans over my ass.*

-Cobie to Dante

Cobie

*Dante dropped down to one knee, and I immediately started to
think the worst.*

*"Are you okay?" I breathed, rushing forward to drop down to my
knees beside him.*

He rolled his eyes in exasperation.

*"Stand up," he growled, pushing me to my feet by putting his
hands on my hips. "This can't be done with you down here with
me."*

*Frowning, I was about to question whether he was experiencing
confusion or if he was dizzy, when he pulled out a velvet box.*

*I froze and stared at that velvet box like it was something akin to
an atomic bomb.*

*"I don't know if there's anything I can say to ever take back those
horrible words I said to you four months ago," he whispered, his
eyes on mine. "I know you say you're okay, that you understood,
but I'd never been at a lower point in my life than I was when I
said those words to you. I didn't mean them. I was mad at myself
and the whole fucking world. I was scared of what you were*

making me feel, and how I was beginning to need you. I've lost my entire world once already... and I just wasn't sure that I could put myself in a position where it could happen again."

He swallowed, the thick lump of his Adam's apple jumping with the movement.

"What I was scared to admit that day was that you had already become my world. You and Mary, you're right here," he pressed his fist against his chest. "You're going to be there forever. You'll have a place inside my heart until I no longer draw breath into my lungs."

A tear slipped down my cheek uninhibited.

He watched it fall, then his eyes returned to mine. "Cobie, will you marry me? Will you live at my side and lend me your strength?"

I nodded. "I'd give you anything you asked for, Dante."

His smile was radiant as he opened the box, pulled out the ring, and held out his other hand for mine. I put my hand in his, and he slipped the ring on my finger.

It was a princess cut diamond, large enough to take my breath away, yet small enough that it wouldn't hinder my movements. It literally flickered like it was filled with an inner light that was meant to attract the eye.

"Dante," I breathed. "It's beautiful."

His smile was small, and as he came to his feet, he pressed his mouth to my own.

"Nothing is as beautiful as you."

The sound of an electric razor had my eyes opening.

I smiled as I threw the covers off of my body and made my way to the bathroom.

Dante wasn't being quiet in his morning routine. But I'd found over the last few weeks since he'd come back to me that he wasn't particularly quiet in anything he did.

Then again, I should've already realized that since I lived with him after my surgery, but I accounted my lack of noticing these things about him to the fact that I was hopped up on the good drugs which allowed me to remain in a semi-conscious state for extended periods of time.

"What put that smile on your face?"

I looked up to see Dante staring at me in the mirror.

"A memory."

That memory would never get old.

Not ever.

He knew which one. He didn't have to ask because my eyes had automatically trailed to the ring on my finger that I never took off.

"You coming to work with me today?"

I rolled my eyes.

I'd done that for the last two weeks. Me and Mary made ourselves at home in the staff lounge.

Now, after two weeks of both of us being there constantly, it was like a second home. Mary had a portable playpen that she used to nap in, and I had blankets that I took over the couch with. All of my shows, as well as Mary's, were on the DVR, and the cabinets were stocked with more than enough snacks to last us while we were there.

Dante would never demand that I stay there, but I knew by his whispered question that he'd feel better having me and Mary close.

Drake still hadn't been found, and until he was, I knew that Dante wouldn't be comfortable if we were out of sight.

Which also explained why I was still on leave from my job.

I still had two months left on my extended leave of absence from my illness until the hospital would no longer be required to hold my position for me, and I knew that I wanted to go back at some point.

I loved Dante. I loved this life that we were building. But I didn't want to be a kept woman. I wanted to do what I loved—and what I loved to do was watch babies being born into this world.

Speaking of babies, the one inside of me started to flip and twirl, making me laugh and press my hand to my belly.

I'd been feeling the movement for weeks now, but it never got old, feeling him press against my hand.

A work-roughened hand joined my own, and I looked up to find Dante standing so close to me that I could feel his body heat seeping into my own.

"Active again," he murmured, his hand touching my belly.

Through Dante's old blue T-shirt that I'd worn to bed the night before, I could see my belly bouncing and jolting with each kick and punch.

"Always active," I corrected, then pushed past him to go to the en-suite bathroom.

I still closed the door. I wanted to leave a little magic in our relationship so I wouldn't be shattering the illusion any faster than I had to.

As far as he was concerned, I didn't poop or pee. I was the exception to that baser human instinct.

He may have helped me do both in the beginning of our relationship when I was recovering here after my surgery, but that didn't count since we weren't together.

When I came out and washed my hands, I had to roll my eyes at the fact that the bathroom counter was covered in beard hair. This bathroom had double sinks, but Dante couldn't seem to figure out which part of the counter was his.

After proposing, Dante had shaved his beard.

Not just a trim, either, but a lot—all of it, in fact.

All of it except for a tiny bit of scruff that lined his jaw and upper lip thanks to the trimmer not being able to get quite close enough.

I kept waiting for him to break out a razor and shaving cream, but he never went that far.

My guess was that the beard had represented a part of his life that he was trying to step away from, but I'd never wanted to confirm that assumption.

I just smiled, silently mourned the loss of his beard, and went about my life with Dante.

We did everything together. We talked. We spoke on the phone. We had dinner together almost three-quarters of the time. We were solid, confident in our relationship and knew what we meant to each other. We were our second chance at life and happiness, and we weren't wasting it.

He wasn't there because he was being forced to be—he assured me of this every single morning—he was there because he wanted to be.

"Come on, it'll be fun."

I looked at him, studying his eyes, and raised my brows. "I missed the question."

"I said, I think we should go on a vacation before you start back to work." He paused. "Travis, his wife and kids, my mother and father, Baylor and his wife and kids, Reed and Krisney and their kids, and a few of the other guys from work have decided to go camping. I want to go to the RV place tonight to go look at a camper. I was asking if you wanted to go. I convinced you that you should, and you said it'd be fun."

I rolled my eyes.

"I'll go if we bring Mary with us," I tried.

At first, I thought it was because Drake was still at large, but then I saw the way people watched Mary when we'd been at the grocery store last week.

Mary, although an absolutely beautiful child, did have Down Syndrome. She was going to attract a few stares anywhere she went. It was sad, it wasn't right, but it was also, unfortunately, the truth. However, I think Dante took it as an insult any time someone stared at his precious girl too long.

Unless they were kids, then he didn't seem to mind.

But, I could tell that he was purposefully keeping her away from any situation where she could potentially be mistreated by someone.

Hence why she never went anywhere with us anymore. If he expected us to go somewhere, he found a babysitter for Mary, usually his mother or one of his brothers.

And that made me sad.

Dante frowned.

"Drake…"

"Dante, we can't keep living our life like this. You have Rafe on us each and every time we leave the house. Sometimes even one of your brothers are there tailing us wherever we go. We can't keep going on like this. You're going to have to allow us some room to breathe. We'll do whatever you want us to do, but we can't live our lives this way indefinitely."

Dante didn't have anything to say to that, so I didn't say anything either.

Instead, I walked back into our bedroom—yes, ours—and over to the closet.

After tugging down a T-shirt that would just barely cover my belly, I tossed it on the bed and went back to the bathroom to pick up my leggings from the night before.

I only had a few pairs, and it was getting to the point where I'd need to get some new ones—and soon.

Yet another thing that I didn't want to ask Dante. I didn't want him to go to the mall with me but seeing as this was my first pregnancy, I didn't know enough about what I would need or how maternity clothes were supposed to fit to order them online.

The few things that I'd borrowed from Hannah were all too big, and I wouldn't be able to wear them until much later in my pregnancy.

Which left me with T-shirts and leggings for the time being.

Shrugging out of Dante's T-shirt, I tossed it on the foot of the bed and reached forward to grab the clean one.

I had it in my grasp when I felt Dante's hands on my hips.

Instantly I knew that he'd come to a decision.

"I'll allow her to come," he murmured. "But you'll come with Rafe. I'll arrive separately. Just in case."

I grinned and pressed myself back into him, feeling the hardness that always seemed to be present when he was this close to me.

"I love you, Cobie."

My heart felt like it was full to bursting.

"I just don't want y'all to get hurt."

I knew he didn't. Which was why I'd allowed him to wrap us both—Mary and I—in cotton.

"Can we go to dinner, too?"

He squeezed my hips, and then let one go to run his hand up the length of my exposed back.

Then he pushed down in the center of my back, bending me over the bed, and I went without complaint.

"You'll have to do a lot of convincing for me to do that."

I shimmied my hips, and he laughed huskily, causing my pussy to clench with need.

That laugh. That laugh would always get me.

I could be madder than a hornet, and all he would have to do was laugh, making his handsome face break out in a smile, and I'd lose every single bit of attitude. All over a smile.

Why?

Because I was a sucker for the man. All he had to do was share that happiness—the happiness that I'd had a part in bringing out in him—with me, and I was putty in his hands.

The next few moments were a lesson in patience as he stripped off his underwear, followed by mine. Then proceeded to tease me relentlessly with his fingers, followed shortly by his tongue.

By the time he was standing up behind me and pressing his length to my entrance, my legs were already on the verge of collapsing.

He held me up by my hips as he pressed himself inside of me. He didn't stop until he was buried fully inside.

Every single inch of me was filled with him.

"Fuck," I breathed, bracing my forearms on the bed as he slowly started to move in me.

He was slow, oh, so slow.

But it was what I needed. What we both needed.

I bit my lip as he pressed himself deep, twisting his hips.

"God," I breathed.

Dante didn't speak, just continued to fuck me.

His hips would press against my backside for long moments. His pubic hair teasing the pouting, sensitive lips of my sex.

Then he'd pull back, taking my breath with him.

In. Out. In. Out.

By the time I realized I was close, I knew it was going to be big.

The sounds of not just our breathing, but also my wetness and moans filled the air. And before I could even think to warn him of my impending release, it was upon me.

The orgasm was something that I experienced every single time with him. Relentless and all-consuming.

My eyes closed, and I dropped my face into the comforter to contain my scream.

I didn't want to wake the child in the room down from ours. Not yet.

So, I silenced my screams and let him take himself the rest of the way there without much help from me.

He came moments after me, filling me with his seed.

"You're so fucking beautiful," he breathed, running his hand down the length of my spine.

I smiled into the sheets, then pushed up just as he pulled himself back.

I felt his release run down the length of my inner thigh and rushed to the bathroom before it could make too big of a mess.

Once I was cleaned up, I heard the pounding of tiny little feet making their way to our room.

I had to laugh as Mary appeared, peeking around the corner almost as if she knew she was interrupting something.

Luckily her father had heard her coming and had pulled on clothes.

I, on the other hand, hung out in the bathroom while Dante led her out into the hall.

Distantly, I was aware of them heading toward the kitchen. The sink turning on. Cabinets pounding.

And then Dante discussing what to have for breakfast with her.

All the while, I stayed there, naked, standing in front of the bathroom mirror.

I took in my appearance.

The bright pink scars that lined where my breasts had once been were never going to be pretty.

My body was skinny, and my belly poked out almost obscenely, even at five months gestation.

My face was flushed from what Dante and I had just done…but I felt beautiful. Dante made me feel that.

Smiling, I walked away from that mirror, not one hint of embarrassment anywhere in me.

I was proud of my body. Dante loved me and the way I looked.

And I loved him.

I loved his little girl—*our* little girl.

I loved everything about my life now.

Drake was a dark cloud hanging over us…but I just knew that everything would work itself out in the end.

We—Dante and I—had suffered too much loss for it to turn out any other way.

Right?

CHAPTER 26

I am so horny that I'm legitimately worried about your safety tonight.

-Text from Cobie to Dante

Dante

The day went off without a hitch.

I found an RV that I liked—one that would fit us all perfectly.

Drake hadn't magically appeared.

Rafe, however, *had* discovered some new information, though.

Rafe came by after we'd gotten home to explain a few things and discuss it with us.

He learned that Drake had been a military arms distributor of sorts. He was the one who held the merchandise that was stolen from the military until they found a buyer, and then Drake would deliver the merchandise for a cut of the profits.

However, the last shipment that Drake had obtained, he'd apparently stolen from the original thieves. They found the merchandise after I'd unknowingly led them to Drake's fortress, which just so happened to be located beneath Cobie's old place— the same place where he held me captive for months.

Once the merchandise was returned to the military, the government moved forward with officially charging Drake with conspiracy to sell military arms, theft and a bunch of other serious charges that would get him a hefty prison sentence once he was convicted.

Although not the sole person responsible for the theft of the merchandise, he was the only one they had been able to identify so far. So, until he could be found and questioned, he would be the only person charged in what they claimed was a theft of millions of dollars' worth of U.S. military inventory.

Rafe had said that they also suspected that Drake had been involved in over two hundred similar thefts of retired military inventory over the last few years based on the similarities between the cases.

Which meant Drake was in a world of trouble when he finally did surface.

"Dante?"

I blinked at the clock.

"Yeah?"

My eyes were burning, and I wasn't sure what the hell I was doing still up, but I was.

"I have a question."

"Shoot," I said, looking over at the couch beside me.

Mary was asleep on the cushion, curled into the arm of the couch as she hugged one of my tennis shoes to her chest. Why she had one of my tennis shoes, I didn't know. But whatever. If it helped her sleep, I'd give her one of my steel-toed work boots to hold on to. Sleep was our friend around here.

I'd worry about all the dirt she got on her in the morning.

"I need to iron my clothes for tomorrow, and I have a problem."

Tomorrow, we were going to a follow-up appointment with Cobie's oncologist to do a round of tests that would determine if she was cancer free.

I blinked, trying to get the fog of sleep out of my eyes. "Yeah?"

"There's a slug in my iron."

I lifted my fist and rubbed my eyes. "There's a what in your iron?"

"A slug," she answered, confirming that what I heard originally was indeed what she'd meant to say. "I don't know how it got in there, but it's in the little reservoir where you put the water for the steam feature. I tried filling up the reservoir and pouring it back out, but the slug is too fat."

I honestly had no idea what to say.

"Uhhh," I murmured.

"And I don't know what to do. This is a two-hundred-and-fifty-dollar iron. Seriously, I can't throw it away. It steams shit and everything. I don't know what to do!"

She sounded somewhat hysterical at this point.

"Will it still work with the slug in there?"

"Yes," she answered hesitantly. "But what if it dies?"

"Then use it for now, and when I'm not so tired, I'll look and see if I can fix it."

She snorted. "I don't think you can. I've looked all over, and it seems like it's all one piece. I don't think there's any way to get the little water container off of the actual iron. I'm still not sure how the little bastard managed to get in there."

I didn't have anything to say to that.

"You're sure it's a slug?"

In answer, she got up and walked out of the room. Moments later she was back with an iron that did, indeed, have a slug in it.

Hmmmmm. "Imagine that."

Cobie rolled her eyes and put the iron on the table. "I keep thinking about putting salt into it. But I decided against that idea because it'd be just my luck that it would go in there and melt the dang thing. Some weird, gross, thick sludge will probably form in there that'll never come out, and then I'll lose the steam feature on the iron forever."

I stared at her, blinking a few times but saying nothing in reply, because honestly, what could I say to that?

"How about we just buy you a new iron?"

Before she could reply, my phone rang.

I cursed and leaned forward to answer it before it could wake Mary up—who'd been more than fussy today. She had two teeth coming in, and she was not a happy camper.

"Yeah?"

"We have a multi-vehicle wreck on the interstate. They estimate over a hundred cars are involved."

I winced. "Let me get Rafe here, and then I'll head over. What mile marker?"

Once I received the mile marker from Travis, I hung up and immediately called Rafe.

Rafe answered, not sounding tired at all despite the late hour.

"Yes?"

"I have to go to work. Can you come over?"

I heard shuffling, then a female's voice on the other end of the line as he left what sounded like the bed.

"Yeah," he confirmed. "I'll be…"

"You always choose her over me!"

I didn't know what to say to that outburst from the woman on the other end of the line.

Rafe said something viciously, and then I heard a door close.

"Sorry," he muttered. "I'll be there in ten."

Then he was gone, leaving me staring at the phone in surprise.

"What is it?"

"Rafe had a woman with him."

"Janie?"

Was that hopefulness in her voice that I heard?

"From the sounds of it? No, I don't think so. It sounded like another woman. Whoever it was, though, sounded jealous. She wasn't very happy that I called and he was leaving."

"Hmmm," she said, sounding disappointed.

Ten minutes later I placed a goodbye kiss on Cobie's lips as Rafe walked through my door.

After getting in my truck and pulling up my alarm app to ensure it was once again set, I walked out and never once thought that I was leaving my new little family with danger lurking around the corner.

Because had I known what was waiting for them, I would've never left.

I would've stayed.

I would've never done what I did next.

CHAPTER 27

A body like this doesn't happen overnight. It takes the college years, pregnancy, neglect, and three extra tacos.

-Cobie's secret thoughts

Cobie

"Wakey, wakey, eggs and bakey," I cooed, tugging lightly on Mary's big toe.

She pulled it away from me and then snuggled down into the couch.

Rafe started to laugh.

"Shut it," I snickered, bending down to run my finger along the length of Mary's foot. "If you don't wake up, Mary Me, you won't get a yummy breakfast. That means cereal."

I sang the last words to her, thinking it would rouse my sleeping beauty, but it didn't.

She just pulled her foot away again when Rafe stood up from his position.

One second I was standing beside the couch, staring down at Mary who'd refused to let go of Dante's tennis shoe, and the next I was falling backward.

Glass shattered, the world around me sounded like it'd exploded, and I was disoriented.

I couldn't figure out what to do, I wasn't sure where I was. Hell, I could just barely manage to breathe.

I was so confused, and I couldn't remember anything.

Distantly I was aware of another bang, this one much sharper than the last.

Then I felt my body moving.

It took me a long time to finally come back to myself, and when I did, I was shaking in fear.

I'd never been so scared in my life as I was right then.

"You think I want to do this?" Drake hissed in my face. "I don't. But he's given me no choice."

I looked at him like he was crazy.

I was in a car. Drake was in my face, and I could hear crying—I assumed from Mary—in the car with me. I didn't see Rafe anywhere in the car.

"We're gonna do this, and to make sure you don't accidentally get out..."

He started to duct tape me to the seat. That's when I started to struggle.

I should've started earlier. Should've tried to get away before. However, I knew that any way I tried was going to end badly for me.

"You know what?" He paused in wrapping the tape around me. "This won't look like an accident if I do it like this."

I agreed. Though I wasn't going to tell him that. He didn't need to know I agreed or disagreed.

The man was unhinged at the best of times. At least lately. Ever since he'd found out I was dating Dante, he'd changed into the man that Marianne had described to me.

"Why are you doing this?" I cried.

I felt sick to my stomach, scared beyond belief and on the verge of a total breakdown.

Dante was going to see this, and his world was going to implode for a second time.

Fuck, fuck, fuck!

"You gave me no choice." Drake tightened his hold on my hair. "First, Marianne had to go and steal the life insurance money from our son's death—which I planned out quite perfectly, thank you very fucking much. I sold our house to help pay the debt, but it wasn't enough. I had to make it look like I fucking cared about that cunt by paying for her hospital stay—which also ended up taking away from the money I had saved. Then, I felt like I was finally catching my lucky break when you gave me your house—all that equipment and storage in it allowing me to make money elsewhere by allowing them to use those tools and storing their shit in the shop—charging them more for my services and building my underground bunker with the extra. Storing even more shit for them. Then you went and took that away from me. I had already tried to contest Marianne's will, and fucking Dante shut that down. I tried to get custody of that kid claiming I was the child's father. Not that I would have ever wanted that stupid freak of a kid, but I would've gotten a good payout on her, what with her being disabled and all. Plus, with her mother being dead, I could've gotten something soon. It would've tided me over…but then your stupid freak of a boyfriend's family ruined that for me, too."

That was the first time I'd heard anything about him contesting the will or him trying to obtain legal rights to Mary.

I honestly didn't think even Dante knew about it because he would've told me. That information was a little too important *not* to share.

He growled.

"Well, no more!"

I didn't know what to say.

I didn't know what Drake was involved in. Again, I'd stayed out of that part of the situation that Dante was dealing with because, frankly, I didn't want to know.

But now, I felt lost. Why would he need this kind of money? What was he into that he needed so much this badly and this fast?

"Please," I whispered. "I didn't do anything to you. Mary didn't do anything, either."

"Fuck you, and fuck Mary."

I opened my mouth to say something else, but before I could, something changed in Drake's panicked eyes.

He reached for me.

"We'll just do it this way."

Then he slammed my head so hard against the steering wheel, so fast and hard, that it was the last thing I remembered.

In the darkness, the terror was gone and things weren't as they seemed.

***

Dante

If I never relived the last moments of my wife and childrens' deaths in my dreams, my life would be perfect.

I scrubbed my hands down my face, trying to clear my mind of the last of the nightmare that I had while I tried to catch an hour of sleep on my office couch.

Even now, twenty minutes later, I was still feeling the effects of that chilling dream.

I was driving to make a pick-up before heading home to pick up my girls, and my heart was still pounding.

I relived my worst nightmares in my dreams, over and over again.

Or I should say, I used to before Cobie came into the picture.

Now, though, I had a woman who woke me when the shadows crept in.

Then again, that woman did a lot of things for me I was just now realizing.

For instance, washing my clothes. Once she learned that Lily used to do it the same way as she did, Cobie changed up her habits. She started folding them differently than she had been doing for years just so I didn't have a reminder of that loss whenever I looked at my folded clothes. She didn't do this because I had asked her to or because she didn't want me to remember Lily, but because she was trying to slow the barrage of memories in an attempt to make sure I didn't have fucking panic attacks.

Then there was the way she completely rearranged her life to revolve around mine. She kept Mary while I worked days and nights and whenever in between. I didn't ask her to take over Mary's care—she naturally stepped into the role of her mother because she wanted to and because she loved Mary as much as I did.

I was so focused on how Cobie cured me of some of my demons that I didn't see the car that was stalled on the side of the road until I'd nearly missed it.

"Shit." I slowed down.

Then I backed up and stopped until the truck's hitch was inches away from the car's bumper.

I'd done this so many times over the years that it was ingrained in me where I needed to stop to make it easiest to hitch up the car.

Getting out, I hooked it up in a matter of moments, secured the vehicle, and then was back in my truck a few minutes after I'd parked.

My phone was ringing when I got back inside, momentarily confusing me.

It was so late at night that nobody should be calling me. Dispatch would call, sure, but they'd do that on my radio, not on my personal phone.

Hitting the answer button without looking at who it was, I placed it to my ear.

"Hello?"

"Finally!"

I frowned and pulled the phone away from my head, looking at the display.

Cobie?

"Who is this?"

"It was so fuckin easy."

A cold chill slithered down my spine.

"Who is this?" I repeated.

"Your worst nightmare."

Something inside me snapped, and I snarled out, "You have no fucking clue what my worst nightmares are!"

"Oh, but I kinda do."

I started to say something, but the sound of flesh hitting flesh stopped me.

"Don't."

I didn't recognize my own voice.

"Sorry, too late. You ruined me, so I'm gonna ruin you."

Then he started to laugh. "Bet you didn't know that it was me with your wife, too."

Everything inside me stilled. "I'd had a few problems. I was thinking about the kid, and whether I was making the wrong decision leaving him in the back of my car all day. Not like I could do anything. But still."

Bile started to work its way up my throat, and I sat there, frozen, as I tried to decide what to do.

I couldn't hang up and call the cops...that would make it to where I no longer had him on the line. And I knew I needed to keep him on the line.

"Where are you?"

I didn't want to hear anything about what he was talking about, but Drake acted like he didn't hear my question. He continued with his story.

"I ran that kid off the road toward your sister's car. It was an accident, of course. They blamed it on the kid texting and driving, but I was the one who'd caused her to lose control."

And then I heard what sounded like a door opening. Followed by Mary's screams.

"You hear that?"

I put the truck in gear, momentarily forgetting that I had a car semi-attached to the back of my truck, and started to roll forward.

The jerk of the chains on the car had me glancing in the rearview mirror, but I still didn't stop.

"Yes," I confirmed. "Please, don't hurt her."

"Oh, I won't hurt her. Or at least it won't appear like it was me."

And then I heard what sounded like him throwing the phone against something hard. "All right, ladies and gentlemen. Take two, and go!"

And I knew then, exactly what he was going to do.

He was going to make it look like Cobie had driven off the same bridge that my wife and children had died on.

I didn't think.

I didn't do anything but drive.

I was two minutes away.

Two minutes.

I could make it.

They would make it.

It would be okay.

It had to be okay.

CHAPTER 28

*I want to live my life like a bear. Eat when I want
to eat. Sleep when I want to sleep. Kill people
when I want to kill people. You know, bear shit.*

-Rafe's secret thoughts

Rafe

Blood was running freely from the wound on my scalp. It was
running into my eyes, down my cheeks, around my nose, to my
chin and then down my neck.

I was fairly sure I had a broken collarbone, as well as a concussion.

But I managed to drive behind Cobie and Mary's captor, Drake.

I'd somehow managed to stay hidden.

I'd even managed to call for help so I could stay where I was.

Because I sure as hell wasn't fooling anyone—not even myself.

I knew the moment that I got out of this car, I'd collapse onto my
knees.

I knew, without a shadow of a doubt, that my legs would give out,
and I'd crumble to the ground in a useless heap.

Did that stop me from getting out of the car, though?

Hell no.

It sure as fuck didn't.

It also didn't stop me from running—or more likely limping, but I wasn't quite sure—toward the bridge where Drake had just pushed Cobie's car off the bridge.

It hit the water below with a huge splash, and I vaguely watched as Cobie returned to consciousness when the jolt of the car hitting the water jarred her awake.

I'd just reached the bridge when I heard, rather than saw, a large truck heading toward us.

Just as I made the decision to jump, I saw a truck pass—a car on a chain directly behind it—headed straight for Drake who was now laughing.

He'd seen me, and he saw the state he'd left me in back at Dante's. He knew just as well as I did that I was about to make the last decision I'd probably ever make.

I had just enough left in me to get them out. I knew I did.

I'd make it happen.

I would.

Over the side of the bridge I went, hitting the water feet first.

The cool water, a huge contrast from the humid air, washed over me, reviving me.

I swam toward the car, which had hit the creek landing on all four wheels. It was slowly settling into the water coming up to the middle of the windows.

I didn't go to Cobie's seat. I went to the back seat and started to yank on the door.

"The locks! Unlock it!"

Cobie's head turned, and she hit the locks.

The moment the door was unlocked, I yanked at the handle, pulling with everything I had to get the door open.

It didn't so much as budge.

***

Dante

Drake's body didn't even hit the pavement after the car I had attached to my truck plowed into him before I was out of the truck.

I dove over the side of the bridge, hitting the water so hard on my stomach that it momentarily stole the breath from my lungs.

I didn't really notice, though, as I swam with the current toward the slowly filling car.

I had a crowbar in my hand, so the strokes were less than elegant as I sliced through the water.

Rafe had one foot planted in the riverbed and the other braced against the car's doorframe as he pulled, and I tapped him on the shoulder.

"Back up."

Rafe, blood running into his eyes, did as I asked.

I didn't spare him another look as I took the crowbar to the back window.

It broke with one swift pop.

Glass shattered inwardly, pelting not just my baby girl with glass, but Cobie as well.

Cobie was already in the back seat, pulling Mary free of her car seat.

I didn't miss the way her movements were slowing.

Her head was bleeding, too.

She handed me Mary, and instead of taking just her, I yanked them both out.

Cobie came willingly, but Mary had clutched onto me with a death grip around my throat, and I wouldn't have been able to let her go if I tried.

I turned away from the car and trudged through the water carrying the two—three counting our baby—most precious people in my life to the river bank.

It was only when I was placing them on the grass that I turned and saw Rafe was nowhere in sight.

CHAPTER 29

Surely not everybody was Kung Fu fighting?

-Cobie to Dante

Dante

Six hours later, they were dragging the river.

Four hours after that, they called a halt in the search until daylight returned.

***

The five men and one woman standing in front of me looked exhausted.

As exhausted as I felt, yet here we all were.

I was standing in the hospital corridor.

"Daddy," Janie pleaded. "His phone is about six miles downstream. I swear to God, he's there."

Janie's father, James, looked at his daughter with sad eyes.

"They've already swept that area, Janie. He's not there."

"He has to be there," she replied stubbornly.

I felt a cold hand slip into my own, and then Cobie wrapped herself around my body.

She'd gone to get us some coffee and something for Mary to snack on when she woke.

Mary was in my brother's arms in the waiting room, and Cobie had stopped there with her spoils before finding me.

She handed me my coffee, and I gratefully took a sip before wrapping my arm around her shoulders and pulling her close.

The last ten hours had been bad.

So bad, in fact, that when Mary, Cobie, and the baby got checked out, I'd gotten checked out, too.

I had been having pains in my chest. I was still not fully recovered from the rhabdomyolysis. My electrolytes were still a little out of balance, but the ER doc said the pain in my chest was likely due to the stress over the last few hours, but I was to be careful.

Hence why I nearly choked when I tasted the decaf coffee Cobie had somehow thought she could slip by me.

I looked down at my woman, and she batted her eyelashes at me. "They said no coffee or anything that'll cause you undue stress for two weeks."

I didn't have anything to say to that, so I didn't.

Instead, I turned to stare at Janie, who was now openly crying.

"Fine," Janie snapped, pushing away from her father. "I'll do it myself."

James followed after her, leaving the four remaining men of Free standing in front of me.

"Did you hear Drake's confession?"

I gritted my teeth.

I had.

I'd been standing in the hospital doorway as he laid out his plan—which was to have a reduced sentence for kidnapping and attempted murder—if he gave up the four men who were involved with him in this scheme to steal retired inventory from the military and resell it.

Four men who were not only still active duty, but were also high-ranking.

"Kind of hard to understand him through his broken jaw."

I looked over at Sam, who was staring at me with open appreciation.

"I didn't much think about it," I told him. "I just saw him standing there, and meant to knock him into the water. I didn't much remember that I had a car barely attached to the back of my truck until it was swinging around to cut off his exit. And by cutting off his exit, I mean it was slamming into him. He's lucky all he got was a concussion and a broken jaw."

"What we do know is that the ADA—assistant district attorney—is going to give him that deal. They really want to know who exactly is behind these thefts. They didn't just stop at guns and old inventory. They've stolen military secrets and intel that could lead to world war three if we're not careful," Max muttered, his eyes on the door down the hall where Janie and James had disappeared.

"I don't know…"

A loud 'CODE BLUE' call sounded over the loudspeaker above our heads.

Cobie stiffened beside me.

"What does that mean?" I asked just as we saw a ton of doctors and nurses running into Drake's room.

"That's the crash team," Cobie murmured, her eyes on the scene down the hall. "That's the team that comes around when a patient has either lost a pulse or is straight up dead."

A doctor came rushing chaotically out of the room, his white coat flapping behind him in his haste to move, and rushed through the door of the stairwell.

The same door that Janie had pushed through a few moments earlier.

The elevators at our sides chimed, and I turned just in time to see Rafe stumble out of the doors before they closed.

I let go of Cobie in my haste to catch him before he fell.

I wasn't successful.

Rafe fell in a heap at my feet, and I rolled him over to his back just in time to see his eyes roll back into his head.

"Oh, fuck."

Cobie was down on her knees beside me, pressing her hand against his throat, and cursing all in a matter of seconds.

"Dante, go get help!"

I did as she'd asked, hurrying in the direction of the nurses' station that was right past Drake's commotion-filled room.

But what I saw as I passed—a doctor calling Drake's time of death—wasn't reassuring.

***

"Do they expect him to be okay?"

I looked over to find Cobie standing beside me, but she answered the young woman's fear-filled words with brutal honesty.

"He had no recollection of what happened, how he got here or even his own name when the doctors asked," Cobie replied gently.

"Will he be okay? Yes. Will he regain his memory? I believe he will, eventually. For now, though? We just don't know if when he wakes up, his memory will have returned. He has a brain bleed from the concussion of the stun grenade that went off in our house. It affected the part of his brain that controls memory. So it's likely, at least for a while, that he won't remember anything."

With that, Janie turned to go into Rafe's room, leaving me alone in the hallway standing with Cobie.

I dropped my head down to hers.

"This was a bad day," she whispered.

It had been.

I couldn't even put voice to the words that churned through my brain.

Scared. Frantic. Thankful.

I was feeling everything all at once, and I couldn't freakin' breathe when I thought about it too hard.

"I'm sorry."

I pulled back and looked down at my woman.

"For what?"

"For… not protecting her better."

I framed her face.

"When I was in basic training, they gave us training on how to handle a stun grenade attack without losing all of our focus on our surroundings," I told her. "It wasn't easy. Even the best of soldiers became disoriented. You, my dear woman, did everything that you could've done under those circumstances. I don't blame you, and I don't blame Rafe. I blame Drake." I blew out a breath. "I just want to put this behind us. With Drake gone, and everybody accounted for and on their way to being okay… I want to just be us. I want to enjoy my life with you. I want to be fucking over the moon and sharing the fact that our baby is the size of a fucking banana or avocado. What I don't want to be doing is living in the past. The past is just that—the past. I'll always be thankful for it, but it's time for me to take a step into the future."

Cobie's hand went to my face, and she pulled me down to brush a kiss against my lips.

"I think I can do that."

I growled against her lips. "Good."

EPILOGUE

*I'll do anything with you except downhill sports
and butt stuff.*

-Text from Cobie to Dante

Dante

One year later

"You're pregnant?"

Cobie was busy throwing up in the toilet, so she didn't answer me.

I just looked at the test on the counter next to where she was and shook my head. "But how?"

"You do know how babies are made, right, D?"

I flipped my brother off. "Yes, Travis."

My brother nodded. "Okay. Just checking. I didn't want you to make this mistake again."

I grinned. "Believe me, this is no mistake, fucker."

Travis's grin was wide as he offered me his hand. "I'm glad you're back."

I took his offered hand and shook it hard, squeezing it like only a big brother could.

"Fuck you," Travis growled, shaking his hand out as he pulled away.

Cobie slammed the door closed, effectively closing us both out, making Travis smirk.

I chuckled as I pulled my hand back and wrapped my arm around Travis's shoulders.

"Since you're here," I started, leading him out into the kitchen. "There's something I wanted to talk to you about."

Travis didn't stop until he was picking up our son, Dante Junior, whom his big sister and his mother called Junior.

Travis brought Junior up to his face and inhaled, just like I sometimes did, and smiled.

"What?"

Travis turned his face to me as he cuddled Junior to his chest.

"Selling you my half of the business so I can start a new one, here in the Longview/Kilgore area."

His eyes went up in surprise, then lowered.

"Why do you have to sell at all?" he questioned. "Why not just open another place?"

I thought about that for a long moment then shrugged. "I guess I kind of thought you'd want something that was all yours."

He started shaking his head. "No. I don't want that. Hannah and I don't want that. We want to keep doing it like we're doing it. I wouldn't mind having a reason to come up here and visit more often."

I grinned.

After the shit that went down with Drake at my old place, we'd never gone back.

My mother, father, and brothers had packed up the house without our help and brought all of our belongings here, to Cobie's place that her grandfather had left her.

Cobie and I started our new life here, but every day I still drove down to Hostel to go to work.

Which gave me a lot of time to think as I drove, and what I came up with was an idea to start up a new business here. Not only to save time but also to give Travis the opportunity to have his own business if he wanted it.

It'd been Cobie's idea to use the sale of her old place—which had sold for a considerable amount of money thanks to Drake's additions to the place—to pay for the start-up of the new business.

I'd thought it was a great idea, mostly because I knew that we wouldn't use that money for any other reason.

In the six months since it sold, the money had just sat in an account earning interest since neither of us had felt it was right to touch it. Me, because it wasn't my house or money to use. Cobie, because she didn't want to make money off of a house where I'd been held captive and tortured.

We only came to the decision to use the money to start the new business last night.

Which had been why I'd invited my brother here in the first place.

What I hadn't expected was to announce Cobie's pregnancy—even though I'd already been thinking that she was.

Over the last week, she'd changed. It wasn't the usual signs, though, but the fact that she'd been a whole lot clingier than normal.

When I'd left to go on a run today, she'd been waiting for me to get back. And had started crying in my arms before I'd even managed to close the door.

"Did he say yes?"

Cobie emerged, face pale and looking a bit green around the gills.

"He said no," Travis said.

"What did he say no for?"

That was Reed, walking through my door without even a knock.

"He said no to allowing them to start a new business in a place that'll keep them away from us," Travis said.

Reed snorted and walked in, holding out his hands for my son.

Travis shook his head. "Go find your own baby."

Reed rolled his eyes and then turned his face in the direction of Cobie. "Did you tell him?"

Cobie looked sheepish.

"Yes."

"You knew?"

Reed was an OB/GYN, but he was not, however, the doctor that had delivered Junior.

There was only so much I could take, and my brother seeing my wife's vagina wasn't one of those things.

"Yep," Reed confirmed. "I was the one who told her to test. I tried to get her to come into my office, but since I was the only one working today, she refused. Said she'd wait for my partner."

I grunted. "Good."

Reed rolled his eyes again.

Reed had not taken the news of Drake's involvement in everything that happened to me well. He'd felt terrible at first, and it was only recently that he had started to return to his old self.

I'd felt bad for keeping him in the dark now because it'd come as a surprise that his oldest childhood friend had been the mastermind behind his brother's agony over the last few years.

The door opened and closed again, then the pounding of feet sounded as Mary ran her way inside, followed shortly by both of my parents.

"Mama!"

Cobie scooped Mary up in her arms and buried her face in our girl's neck.

I grinned inwardly, but outwardly I scowled. "Hey, what am I, chopped liver?"

Mary's giggling face popped up, and she stuck out her tongue.

My brothers chuckled.

My mom patted my chest. "Maybe the next baby will like you better."

Then she walked over to Travis and stole Junior from his arms.

Travis scowled.

Reed grunted. "I was next!"

And I was left feeling utterly euphoric at having my family surrounding me.

I was no longer sad all the time.

Sure, I had my moments sometimes when a memory would hit, or something would catch my eye that reminded me of Lily or the girls.

But mostly, they were good memories now. Memories that left me feeling happy and smiling rather than broken and raw.

And, as more and more of my family came in to celebrate Mary's birthday, I realized that my life, although not how I once thought it would turn out, was exactly what I needed it to be.

It was my kind of perfect.

***

In an hour, Mary's best friend, Dobbie, showed up.

Dobbie, the little boy that Cobie had taken care of during clinicals in nursing school, was no longer just a part of Cobie's life, but Mary's and mine as well.

I also didn't like the way Mary looked at him—as if he was her whole world.

"You better watch out, Daddy." Cobie came up from behind me. "That's looking a lot like love."

I lifted my arm and wrapped it around her.

"Don't even think about it."

She snickered into my shoulder. "My lips are sealed."

ABOUT THE AUTHOR

Lani Lynn Vale is married to the love of her life that she met in high school. She fell in love with him because he was wearing baseball pants. Ten years later they have three perfectly crazy children and a cat named Demon who likes to wake her up at ungodly times in the night. They live in the greatest state in the world, Texas. She writes contemporary and romantic suspense, and has a love for all things romance. You can find Lani in front of her computer writing away in her fictional characters' world...that is until her husband and kids demand sustenance in the form of food and drink.

Made in the USA
Monee, IL
15 January 2020

20391114R00167